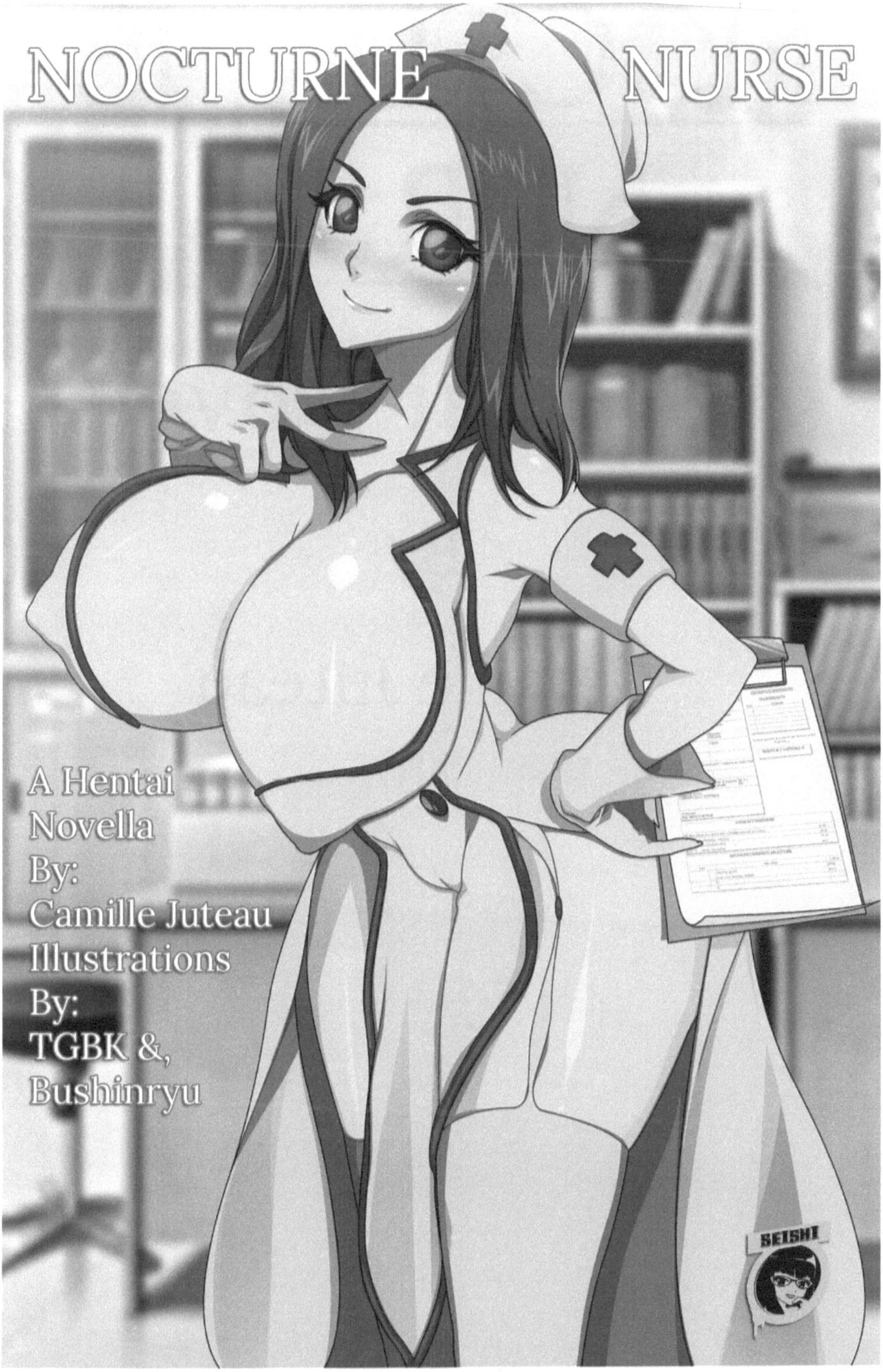
NOCTURNE NURSE
A Hentai Novella
By:
Camille Juteau
Illustrations
By:
TGBK &,
Bushinryu
SEISHI

NOCTURNE NURSE

A Hentai Novella

By

Camille Juteau

COPYRIGHTS

ISBN Numbers:
ISBN Number For eBook (Electronic Book) version:
978-0-9958398-3-0

ISBN Number For Paperback (Physical) version:
978-0-9958398-4-7

CREDITS

Original Concept & Story By: Camille Juteau

Illustrations By:

TGBK (Cover Art)

Bushinryu (Other Illustrations)

Editor: Kellie O'Reilly

Produced By: Seishi

Table of Contents

PROLOGUE

There she was, running, in the wild, in the cold of the night, with her huge, flopping tits moving in the air. She was escaping. Desperately fighting for her life as her assailant was stalking her into the night.

This young woman had been a nurse in the past, it was meant to be her vocation. She knew it. She was a healer. Except that she wasn't anymore, she had stopped this practice some time ago and this was the reason she was being chased down the street in her own hometown.

Someone came for her. Or rather something came for her. A masked figure with a doctor coat, not a normal one, it was darker, almost black. It was wearing a mask with medical red crosses for its eyes, replacing them in a terrifying way. Its mouth was made of stitches as if its smile was broken, injured at some point prior to this event but fixed. The mask itself was black, a devoid of life and light facade.

This woman was on her way back home when she was attacked out of nowhere by this slasher, this masked attempted murderer. She was only feet away from entering her apartment building before the man sprung out of the darkness of the area. She already had her keys in hand; she was ready to enter her home, where she would have been safe. She would have been definitely safer at least, safer than outside, out in the wild.

It was late. It was past midnight. It was cold. It was winter. Snow was everywhere. Not a chat was there outside; no one was there to help her. With the entrance to the apartment building unavailable and blocked by the man, she circled the area. She ran, went around the building. She circled it until she soon enough arrived back at the entrance of the door. She found the strength and the courage to yell for the first time as she saw the light near the entrance. She screamed her guts out, she screamed for help.

"HELP. HELP. ANYONE, PLEASE, HELP."

It was Friday night, so she knew probably no one was currently present in the building she lived in. One person lived in the building with her, chances he was not there was pretty high. In addition, as usual, most of her neighbors had already left for the weekend. They went away for adventurous trips. She had no indication that help was around, but her apartment building was still the place she decided to go to. She thought her home was the safest place she could go to right now and this was where she rushed herself to.

But sadly for her, she fell down on the cement ground, inches away from the glass doors. She had even felt the touch of one of the two steel handles during her fall. She quickly touched the handle which meant she was so close to maybe be out of trouble. She fell down on the ground on the side of her body, her left hip and shoulder both took most of the hit. Her big breasts crashed and bounced on the ground following the fall.

The bright yellow light of the entrance spot illuminated the young woman. It was significant; it was the first time she was not hidden in darkness. Her beautiful face was finally visible in the night. She had large and extremely cute almond coloured eyes. She had a beautiful nose and glamorous, peachy lips. Despite the horrible situation, her cheeks seemed so charming and sexy with the cute, wide shape they had. Her long hair was light brown and ended around her shoulders. She had pale white skin. Despite her very short height and her skinny frame, her breasts were huge. The exact size of her boobs was: thirty K. She also had large hips and a big ass. She wore a thick sweatshirt and pair of jeans. She didn't currently show a lot of skin with her clothes. And it felt right as well. It was a cold night, colder than she originally thought it would be. She needed to be well dressed. She also wore a pair of cotton gloves and brown boots.

After her fall, she almost immediately turned her head around and took a quick look behind her. The man with the two red crosses mask was there, on her heels, never stopping to stalk her into the night for one second. She quickly got up and opened one of the two glass doors at the entrance of the building.

The man attempted to catch her before she went inside, it tried to reach her arm with its hand but closely failed to do so. With her keys still in the palm of her hand (thanks to her taking it out of her pocket a few minutes ago), she used her keys to lock to two doors. It was an emergency key given to her by her landlord; the other tenant of this building received one as well.

She did it. She had successfully locked the doors before the man could even try to open them. But it didn't stop there, the young woman showed a victorious smile for a short moment.

She grabbed her cell-phone from one of the pockets of her coat and typed: 'nine-one'. She was about to type the last remaining: 'one' when the stranger stole her attention from the other side of the doors, freezing her, preventing her from calling for help right away.

The attempted murderer delicately placed its fingers on its mask. He slowly but surely started to remove it from its face. Underneath it, the stranger revealed something else hiding its identity and its face – a tablet, a Samsung Galaxy Tab tablet – after fully removing the mask, it clicked on the power button to turn on the device. It then touched the touch screen, clicked on the 'play' option of a video. The video started.

The video was the self, cell-phone recording of this young woman. This was the recording of her filming herself in a bathroom. She was wearing something entirely different, as real blue and white nurse outfit. This was a very kinky recording; the woman in the video was all playful, smiling a lot. This looked like a booty filming. The woman showed her huge cleavage.

"I heard you wanted to date a nurse. Is that right? Here I am. Just for you. But if you want me, you've got to keep this video to yourself only. Right, can I count on you, honey?"

The kinkier version of this woman said on the tablet. This smile quickly disappeared as she saw the video she filmed herself, probably a long time ago. She was frozen for now. She only had two more touches to do to call nine-one-one but she couldn't bring herself to do it just now. It *had* her attention, she was distracted.

" Nobody will see this except you, nobody, and nobody..."

The video kept playing.

CHAPTER ONE

She was safe inside the building, behind the glass doors, safe for now. The stranger was standing still, observing her outside. Being directly shown the kinky video she filmed herself in the past didn't stop her to call for help. The young woman had pressed on the final: 'one' she had to press on to dial: 'nine-one-one'. She then finally called.

Ring. Ring. Ring.

"Nine-one-one, what is your emergency?"

"Thank God, this guy is trying to kill me, he chased me down to my home."

"Alright, what is your address ma'am?"

Meanwhile, the stranger punched one of two glass doors using its fist. It was so strong its first and only punch pierced a huge hole into the glass. Fissures, cracks, the hole is large enough it can fully slide its arm inside. And it did. The intruder soon unlocked the doors. It pushed them. It was now inside the building.

The young woman immediately turned around and ran upstairs using the staircase. She kept talking with the lady on the phone during her rush in the stairs.

"Seven-thirty-eight, apartment four on Shadow Heart street, Thunder-Falls..."

She yelled out to her. Before leaving the stranger downstairs, she had just enough time to hear the video continuing to play.

"Nobody will see this except you my, love."

And then, the intruder placed the dark mask back on its face, or rather, back on the tablet. The screen getting covered didn't stop the device from continuing to play the perverted video. The audio of it kept going no matter what, no matter how much the stranger moved and ran very fast once inside the building.

"Do you want me to remove my nurse uniform?"

The young woman's voice was heard behind the scary mask. It oddly made the attempted murderer seemed like the girl's voice was its voice but of course, wasn't.

***

Once upstairs, the woman instantly went to get help from her neighbour, her only neighbour, the only other person inhabiting this building in addition to her. His name was Mr. Rogers. Mr. Samuel Rogers. The girl assaulted his apartment door, she first tries to open it but it was locked. She then hit it multiple times very hard with both of her hands. It sadly didn't help her.

"ROGERS, ROGERS, OPEN UP, LET ME IN."

She yelled at the door, screamed in pure terror. It didn't seem to help either. Mr. Rogers sadly never responded to her. It didn't prevent her from trying some more. She hit at the door with her right fist and tried to turn the doorknob with her left hand. But in addition of the door being locked – the steel of the doorknob progressively became warmer and warmer – to the point of becoming boiling hot, burning hot. The woman had to stop touching it; she even burnt her hand a little. She screamed in pain.

Smokes started coming out of under Mr. Rogers's door. It was now pretty obvious that a fire had been ignited. Her neighbour's apartment was burning, it was on fire. Mr. Rogers was in grave danger.

"Rogers, ROGERS GET OUT OF YOUR APARTMENT RIGHT NOW. THERE IS A FIRE."

But then, before the woman could do anything to try to save her neighbour, the man in the red crosses mask mystically appeared behind her. It silently approached, quietly walking, moving through the intense smoke. It raised its arm in the air; it was not holding a weapon but rather a syringe. It went around her as she still tried to burst open the door. The man pricked the tip of the syringe in her neck, injecting something into her.

This was when she fell unconscious. She was gone.

***

During her sleep, she remembered something that happened to her before. She remembered what the man in the red crosses mask made her see on the screen of the tablet on his face. She remembered the time she was *'hiding'* in one of the washrooms in the hospital she was working at. She was no longer an employee of this place. But at the specific time she took and self-filmed the video that was shown on the tablet, she was a nurse. She was working as a nurse at this hospital. And instead of working there, she was basically more or less wasting her time filming a kinky video for her boyfriend of the time. A boy that she was definitely separated from some time ago, it didn't last forever. In addition to being recorded, this video was live-streamed directly to her boyfriend. He often private messaged his girl during the streaming of the video, encouraging the young woman to go further and further.

"Nobody will see this except you, my love. Do you want me to remove my nurse uniform?"

She said to her boyfriend, teasing him. She smiled at the camera of her cell-phone, smiling to him.

Yes, honey. More, more, show me more.

The boyfriend responded through messaging. She then accepted. She gladly accepted. She kept unzipping the center zipper of her blue and white nurse uniform. She unzipped it till it was full unzipped, therefore, revealing most of her chest. She took off the top of her nurse uniform showing her boyfriend progressively more and more of her body. Her aqua coloured bra was the only thing preventing him from seeing the glory of her big breasts, her thirty K tits. Her almond coloured eyes pierced through the camera of the cell-phone, definitely becoming a highlight of the private show. Her boyfriend could gaze into her eyes, making eye contact as his camera was also turned on. Her light brown hair ended in her immense cleavage as she slowly undressed for her loved one. The sparkling colour in her hair made a great combination with her very pale skin; it made her hair popped a lot.

"How's that, my love?"

Good. Very good, could I see your big udders now?

She didn't even take the time to remove her bra; she simply, softly pulled one of her tits out of it. She pulled her boob out of her bra and revealed it to

12

her man. She intentionally made it bounce in the air to add to the sexual excitement. It bounced up and down for a few seconds.

"Like this?"

Um, yes, may I see the other one now?

"Well, not quite, not right now, I want to show you something else first."

What is it?

She then slowly panned down the camera of her cell-phone and showed him her crotch. Surprise, she had already pulled down her underwear off screen, hiding it from her boyfriend until now. Her filthy pussy was naked, unveiled, one-hundred percent revealed to him.

"Just a little something for you..."

Um, very intersecting, I see, so, you've been hiding things from me to grant me this surprise, huh?

She moved her fingers down to her crotch and used them to open up her vagina. She opened it very wide, showing him the inside of it.

"Of course, I planned this out in advance for you."

Good because I had planned something for you as well. A sort of surprise...

"Really, what is it?"

Look behind you and you'll see.

The boyfriend quickly typed as she kept showing him the interior of her pussy. After finishing reading what he had just sent her as a message, she turned around in the hospital washroom she was currently hiding in to discover her manager, staring at her.

"Miss Lauren Winkler, you're fired, get your stuff and leave."

CHAPTER TWO

The young woman was lying down on a hospital bed. She was just rushed into the emergency room. She had been unconscious, asleep for some time now, probably a little over an hour or so. Only a few minutes after arriving into the emergency room, Lauren Winkler slowly but surely opened her eyes. She was deeply confused, everything seemed very confusing to her. Her eyes were only half-opened, yet, she could still see most of what surrounded her during her awakening.

Plenty of doctors and nurses were in the emergency room with her. She was surrounded by people constantly walking around and visibly stressfully communicating with each other. To her, the doctors and the nurses seemed more like hard-working ants than actual people. She had the strange feeling to be trapped in an ant farm.

She had no idea what she was doing here. Why was she in a hospital? Was this the hospital she was still working in a few weeks ago? It looked like it to her at least. This room looked like the same emergency room she had stepped in a million times before during work. Speaking of emergency room, why was she here? What was so urgent? What was so urgent about her? Was she injured? She had no idea. She had a lot of trouble remembering what recently happened that night. She didn't even remember a single thing that happened today or yesterday as well.

Minutes later, she had found some more strength in her. Lauren was finally able to open her eyes wider. Or, at least one of them, her left eye remained half-opened while she was fully able to open her right one. She was naturally able to see clearer. She noticed that she was no longer wearing her thick sweater. It had been removed from her. She would have been entirely topless if it was not of the bra that remained on her. With time, she could gradually hear better as well. It was very complicated for her to make out what the doctors and the nurses were actually saying, but she could hear a few words.

"Rohypnol..."

"Roofies..."

Those were some of the words she kept hearing as she also noticed that she had plastic tubes all over her body. Something had happened, something was happening, but she had no idea what exactly. Through the crowd of medical personnel, one specific doctor caught Lauren's attention more than the others. It was a young man, way too young looking to be an actual doctor. He seemed to be in his late teens or very early twenties. He had cute yellow eyes and short gray hair. As soon as Lauren laid her eyes on him, he moved closer to her. They made eye contact. He spoke to her. But she couldn't hear him. She could no longer hear anything for some reason. She observed his lips moving without making any sound before she unintentionally fell asleep again.

***

The next morning, Lauren opened her eyes as the early sunlight came into her hospital bedroom through a window. She was awake. The weather seemed great; it was sunny out, no clouds. She first thought she was alone in the room when she looked outside, but no.

"How are you feeling, young lady?"

A masculine but quite young voice said. Lauren turned her head around and saw the same adorable doctor with the yellow eyes she saw last night during her time into the emergency room.

"Good morning, Miss Winkler..."

"You're the boy I saw in the ER, it's you, right?"

"I beg your pardon, 'the boy' you say?"

"I mean, I mean the young man..."

"You would be right. My name is Doctor Ethan Garden and the one that is mainly in charge of you. Before jumping into too quickly into the reasons why you're here, I would like to ask you how you are feeling this morning?"

"I feel good Doctor, I'm ready go home now."

She said while quickly leaning forward, raising her back in the air. Doctor Ethan Garden suddenly stopped her, he stopped her from moving. If he didn't do it, Lauren would have tried to get up from her bed and she would have probably fallen down. He caught her as she slipped down the mattress.

"Miss Winkler, don't try to get up now, it's too soon. You need to rest, you need to recover first."

During her attempt in getting out of the bed, Lauren came out of under her blanket – revealing she was no longer wearing any of the clothes she had when she first got here – she was instead wearing a light blue hospital patient robe. Doctor Garden placed her back in her bed.

"But I'm feeling fine."

"I'm sorry, you stay in bed, it's the protocol, you need to rest. You need to take your time."

A minute of silence split the conversation as she turned her head to the window on her right. She looked outside, distracted herself observing the sky.

"Tell me. What happened to me last night?"

"Do you remember anything?"

"For some reason, back in the ER last night, I couldn't remember anything, but now, *some* of the things seemed to come back to me."

"For example...?"

"I remember coming back from work. I remember a man, a man chasing me. I remember the burning hot doorknob, the smoke, oh gosh, the smoke."

"Miss Winkler, it's not going to be easy, but your apartment burnt down. Your apartment burnt down. You were found unconscious by the firefighters. They saved you just in time before the flames could come too close to you. You were very lucky."

"I still don't remember much. Why was I unconscious?"

"I'm sorry to say, but you were drugged. It was: Rohypnol. A pill with the strong ability to make people fall asleep when consumed. But oddly enough, this drug was given to you through liquid injection on the side of your neck. That's the strange part we are still trying to figure out. I don't want to alarm you or to scare you, but Rohypnol is a drug often used by rapists..."

She immediately interrupted the doctor.

"Oh my God, does that mean I was..."

And he interrupted her back,

16

"No, no, no, not at all, I was just about to tell you. We did our very best to make sure to know if it happened or not, and no. I can assure you: You were not raped."

A beat, Lauren took the time to think before speaking again. She seemed reassured by the doctor.

"Then, why the rape drug...?"

"Unfortunately, I do not have the answer. This is a good question. This is why there will be a serious investigation I assume. You will receive the visit of police officers when you'll feel better."

Doctor Garden slowly stood up from his chair and took his files with him.

"For now, please rest."

He turned around; he walked out of the room. But before he could fully leave, Lauren asked him one more question.

"What hospital is this? The ER almost fooled me last night. But this is *not* the general hospital of Thunder-Falls."

"You're right. This is not the general hospital of Thunder-Falls."

"Then, what is this place?"

"The other hospital of Thunder-Falls..."

"The clinic...?"

"Yes, the medical clinic on Phoenix Avenue..."

The doctor turned around, he went through the doorway. He was off to see his next patient before she stopped him again.

"Where's my phone?"

"It's still with your clothes. Your clothes have been in contact with the smoke of the fire way too much. We need to clean them good before handing them back to you. I'll bring you your phone at the same time, with your clothes."

"Wait, why? What does my cell-phone have to do with the clothes I was wearing last night? I want my phone now. I want to call my family and my friends. I want them to know I'm here. Were they even warned of what happened?"

"..."

The doctor didn't bother giving her more info or speaking any longer to her for that matter. He slowly turned around again and finished walking through the doorway. He was out of her bedroom. As soon as he left the room – Lauren jumped in the air, sprung out of her bed and rushed herself to him – she was about to leave the room as well. She would have had the time to do it, before Doctor Garden pushed a button on the wall of the hallway, activating a transparent glass door. The door quickly slid from right to left, therefore, stopping Lauren in her run. She was trapped in her own recovery bedroom, unable to leave. The two were only inches apart from each other, yet, Lauren felt like she was imprisoned into an underground dungeon.

''Don't worry, Miss, we'll allow you to call your family and friends once you would have gotten some good rest. You shouldn't be up as well. Go back to your bed, alright?''

Lauren was pissed. After being forced to stop her run to get out of the bedroom, she unintentionally crashed into the glass door. Now very intentionally, she placed and pushed with the palms of her hands against the door. The exact same for her head and her breasts. Her forehead was pushing hard against the glass. Her tits were digging into it. Due to her only wearing a patient robe at the moment, her cleavage was heavily showed.

''What kind of hospital is this?''

Doctor Garden then slowly turned around and left in the hallway. Without even saying one more word...

CHAPTER THREE

With no cell-phone with her, no landline phone in her bedroom, and no one to talk to, Lauren was about to go nuts. It wasn't working for her. Despite the previous night that was still mostly a mystery to her, she felt fine. She felt good. She didn't feel sick or injured or anything like that. For her, she was ready to go.

Two hours, forty-two minutes and sixteen seconds after her recent encounter with Doctor Ethan Garden, Lauren couldn't stand the concept of wasting her time here anymore. The amount of time exclusively reserved to think she had for herself might have been useful to her for one thing and one thing only. She had maybe found a way to get out of here. She would use her many charms to perform this escape. During her lonely time, she saw a lot of personnel of this establishment, walking in the hallway. They were nurses, doctors, janitors, and even other patients. Some of them even occasionally looked at Lauren during their walk in the corridor. She would, of course, speak to them, or rather, mostly yell at them in hope to be let out of her *'cell'*, but it never helped. Especially the yelling... Anyway, a lot of men came by her room and this gave her an idea or two.

The clock on the wall of her room kept her well informed on how much time was she left alone to rot. It was now: ten, twelve AM. She was tired of waiting and she was about to make her move. She got out of her bed again and stood up near the doorway, right at the center of the glass door. She now patiently waited for the next man to see pass by.

Um... No, not this one, I need a guy.

She thought when the next person who came in the hallway was a woman. Not that she thought she couldn't score with a woman, but you know? She simply preferred to wait for a man instead; to be sure her plan would work a little better.

And boom. There he was. The man she was waiting for. He was skinny, he was bald, and he looked like a scientist in need of some lust. He was walking fast; he seemed pretty busy and focused on whatever he had to do. She, of course, had to distract him in order to make him stop walking. She had to catch his attention and not let it go.

"Hey, you, wait a minute, please stop."

She yelled at the bald man while quickly pulling up the bottom part of her patient robe. Before he had the time to leave, he turned his head during his walk and saw Lauren, with her chest unveiled to him. It immediately caught his attention and he stopped walking. He turned around and moved to the entrance of her bedroom.

"Me...?"

He said with a curious expression on his face. He smiled while staring at her big, bouncing titties. She kept softly jumping up and down near the doorway.

"Yes, you, I'm sorry for stopping you, I need your help."

Upon his arrival next to her room, she pulled her robe back down, quickly hiding her generous chest. He lifted up his head; he actually looked at her eyes for the very first time. He smiled. She smiled back to him.

"What can I do for you?"

"I need to go to the washroom. It's very urgent."

He leaned forward. He took a look at her room.

"You already have a toilet in there."

"Yeah, of course, I know, I know. But I actually have a problem with it. It doesn't flush well, so I thought I might use another or something."

The bald man clicked on the button on the wall of the hallway and opened the glass door. He entered inside, ran to her personal washroom to go take a look at what the problem could be. He, of course, made sure she came with him to avoid her escaping.

Once in there with her, he tried flushing. Everything worked well, no problem here. He turned to her with a frown on his face.

"Look, I'm sorry for lying to you. I don't understand why I'm being kept imprisoned in this hospital bedroom but I need to go, I'm feeling just fine. I need my phone. I need a phone. I've got to call my friends."

"Lady, you've got to understand, I'm not even supposed to be here with you in your room. You have been placed into quarantine for a reason."

"Quarantine...? Nobody told me about quarantine. Anyway, I've got to go. How about I let you touch *them* and you let me make a phone call? Just so I can call my friends. Okay?"

She proposed to him while lifting up her robe again, showing him all the goods. A long silence took place in the washroom. The two stared at each other for a while.

"I'm sorry. I'm not interested in *them*. I'm gay. But you can still go make a phone call if you really want."

***

Down in the hallway, not too far from her bedroom, the bald man had pointed her location to a landline phone. He stood not too far from her. He was supervising her, making sure she was not escaping or something like that. He was also on the phone. He was on the phone with someone.

Finally, Lauren was very excited to be having access to a phone. Her desire to call for help was immense. Her need to let people she personally knew know she was here was limitless. In addition of the bald woman looking at her in the hallway, the secretary of the clinic also gave her a look from far away. This lady was old and kind of ugly, she'd a big nose. Lauren saw the secretary, noticed her for a second or two and then went back to the numbered buttons in front of her. However, she remembered something important; she remembered she didn't have a lot of family members she could call. She also remembered she doesn't have many friends, if at all. The only *'friend'* that came across her mind was, well... Her ex-boyfriend, the one who manipulated her, lied to her, got her fired from her job as a nurse at the general hospital, and then broke up with her. Yes, that one. She didn't want to call him, but she had no choice. She dialed his number.

Ring. Ring. Ring.

No answer for now. It rang some more.

Ring. Ring. Ring.

Still no answer, he wasn't there or accepting the call.

Ring. Ring. Ring.

He never responded. The call eventually went to his voicemail.

"Hey, I'm not here so please feel free to leave a message."

Beep.

"Hey, it's me, it's Lauren. I know you don't want me to call you, I don't want to call you either but I got a bit of a difficult situation here and I don't know who to call. I don't really know how to say this but my apartment apparently burnt down and I was drugged by someone. I'm at the hospital now. Not the general one but the other one, the medical clinic. I know this is super weird, they don't want to let me go, they say I'm in quarantine. I have no idea why. Anyway, if... When you listen to this message, I would appreciate it if you come here to get me or even at least call me back. Call this clinic and ask for me, alright? Bye."

She hanged up. She immediately started dialing another number. This time, she was calling the police department of Thunder-Falls. She was calling them just in case this clinic didn't tell the cops about where she is. As she was dialing the number – the bad man who was supervising her ended his phone call as well – he dangerously and slowly started walking up to her. Sadly for Lauren, he took the phone off her hands before she could call the police department. He smiled at her again.

"The director wants to see you in his office."

CHAPTER FOUR

It felt like the throne room of a majestic castle rather than a typical hospital director office. It truly felt like a royal place. The two, big, golden doors were about to be opened right before Lauren's eyes. The bald man escorted her; he even grabbed her right arm as they were advancing, slowly moving toward the doors. As they were only a few steps away from the entrance, the doors started opening themselves. They were probably remote controlled; someone had to have opened them on the other side, in the throne room.

"Let me go. I don't need you to escort me. I can walk by myself."

Lauren said to the bald man as the doors were opening. The first thing she saw on the other side was the back of a man sitting on a chair. This man wore a white doctor jacket. He turned around as Lauren and the bald man slowly came inside. It was: Doctor Ethan Garden. He seemed to be having a meeting or at least a conversation with someone else here. Or was he expecting and waiting for Lauren to come?

"Miss Winkler, please come take a seat with us."

The young-looking doctor said to her as they arrived. The bald man escorted her inside and closed the two doors behind them. She turned her head around and took a look at the now closed doors. It felt as if she had just been barricaded in there against her will. When she turned her back to the throne room, she saw the director of this hospital, of this entire medical clinic. At first glimpse, she immediately noticed how much of a handsome man he was. He seemed to be in his fifties, but he probably was in his sixties, to be honest. Nonetheless, he easily could have passed for someone in his forties with the dashing look he had. He had dark green eyes and short James Bond-looking brown hair. He had tanned skin. He was Mexican. He wasn't sitting on his throne; he was standing in front of his large, golden desk. He didn't wear anything that looked like a doctor outfit. He wore a black business suit. He looked like he was eagerly expecting Lauren.

"Welcome Miss Winkler, please make yourself comfortable."

The bald man then attempted to once again escort her somewhere, this time, to a chair right next to Doctor Garden. She got pissed off at him and took back her right arm.

"For the last time, let me go. I can walk."

And she did. She walked to the chair next to Doctor Garden. She sensually walked in front of the three boys, widely stretching her legs, allowing them to see them clearly. She then sat down on the chair, crossed her sexy legs together.

"What is this place? Who are you?"

She directly asked the director. He stayed up as their meeting began.

"My name is Cameron Ross. I am the director of this clinic. Thanks for coming here and allowing us to have a word with you."

"Why do I have the feeling that I was kidnapped by you...?"

"Um... I want to assure you, this is not the case, young lady. Everything is going to be fine but we do need to be honest with you."

"Did you called the police? Do they know what happened?"

"Last night, we received your emergency call. We sent an ambulance. We got you out of your building apartment just in time, before the fire could burn you. Sadly, the entire building burnt down."

"The entire building, completely...? I remember now. My neighbours, Rogers... The smoke was coming from *his* apartment. Is he here? Is he alright?"

"*Rogers...?*"

Doctor Garden curiously asked her.

"My neighbours, Samuel Rogers..."

"The firefighters are *the* ones who got you out of there before we arrive. They said you were the only one in the building that night."

The director told her with a sad but comforting voice.

"He was there. He's probably still there or nearby. They need to save him. I'll go back right now. I need to find him."

She quickly stood up. She was ready to leave. As soon as she stood up in the throne room, Doctor Garden stood up as well. He and the bald man both gathered around her, preventing her from leaving.

"No, not right now, we can't allow you to leave, it's too soon."

24

"You need to stay for now. We'll tell the police about your neighbour."

Doctor Garden and the bald man respectively said. She fought them. She tried pushing them out of her way in order to leave.

"And there is the masked man. He tried hurting me. He's probably going to go after Rogers now."

"Yes, about him, I need to tell you the truth. That's why we can't allow you to leave just now. This man... He's the one who drugged you. You need to know about him."

The director urgently said to her.

"How do you even know this? You weren't there, right? I'm tired of asking you this, but what kind of 'clinic' is this? When I dialed: nine-one-one last night, the general hospital was supposed to come, not you. I was supposed to be hospitalized there, not here. Tell me the truth now."

Cameron Ross stayed silent for a bit. He seemed to be thinking, brainstorming how to reveal the truth to her.

"Yes, you are right. You are absolutely right. We intercepted your call and went to get you after the firefighters saved you from the fire. We brought you here before the other ambulance from the general hospital even could."

The bald man and Doctor Garden stopped trying to keep her in place; they removed their hands from her. She remained motionless for a while as she was processing what the director just told her.

"So, you basically kidnapped me and now you are keeping me here as your prisoner? Why?"

The director then failed to give her an answer. He tried, but couldn't. He seemed to be feeling very bad regarding how things turned out in the end. Following the non-answer he told her, Lauren turned around and left. The two other men were no longer blocking her way. The two big doors opened up by themselves as she moved toward them.

"I'm sorry for what happened to you last night and how we tried to take care of it. I promise you it wasn't our intention to make you a prisoner or anything like that. You are not a prisoner. You are free to go. You can leave whenever you want to. But please don't do it. Stay here. You're at risk..."

This was the limit of what the director could tell her before she had left the room, the two, big doors automatically closing behind her. After her

25

departure, Doctor Garden and the bald man gathered around the director's desk.

”We can't allow her to leave, sir.”

Doctor Garden said to his boss.

”Sadly, we can't do anything. We can't force her.”

Cameron responded to him.

***

It didn't take her very long to leave the throne room, to leave the hallway where her bedroom (or rather her own, little, private cell) was. She walked really fast; she quickly arrived at the entrance of the clinic where the secretary of the establishment was. She didn't let her the time to see her much, Lauren started running. She sprinted as soon as she first saw the doors that led outside. She reached one of them and pushed it with all her strength.

Finally, she was outside. She was out of there, being outside never felt so great and lively to her. Once outside, she stopped running. She pacifically walked and breathed the air around her. She seemed happy.

When she was now exactly ten feet away from the entrance of the clinic, a presence was felt, lurking behind Lauren. It was here. But she didn't know about it just yet. The man in the mask with the red crosses stood behind her, about twenty feet away from her in a park near the clinic. It was staring at her. But she had no idea.

CHAPTER FIVE

Like an apex predator stalking its prey, the man in the mask with the red crosses slowly but surely moved toward Lauren. She was still passively walking on the sidewalk of the street as it started hunting her. She was still only wearing her patient robe, but she didn't care at all. She didn't even think about that small detail at the moment.

It was perfect for it as well; the attempted murderer had it easy. The woods were out. No one was around. Only Lauren and it were in the street near the medical clinic. Each time she made a small step further from the establishment she was recently trapped in, it made a move. It moved closer to her. While very slowly, it extremely dangerously, it stepped closer and closer to her. It somehow felt unusual for this stalker to do this in the middle of the day; it looked a lot like a creature of the night. It probably was as well, it was pretty hard to forget that it had originally appeared during the night when it chased down Lauren near her home. Perhaps it showing itself during the day was a sign of pure obsession for the ex-nurse. Perhaps the need of finding her again was a lot more important to it than waiting for the night to come to hide during the stalking.

Nonetheless, Lauren was now about forty feet away from the clinic. The man in the mask had disappeared for a short moment. It hid and then vanished into thin air behind a couple of trees.

When she thought she was definitely out of trouble, Lauren showed a slim smile on her face. She looked like she was progressively getting better following her *'escape'* from the clinic. She soon stopped getting better when the man suddenly showed up again. It quickly re-appeared behind another tree. Not behind her this time, it was no longer hiding. This time, it had sprung out right in front of her, still carrying the same sharp syringe it was carrying last night. Lauren accidentally bumped into it; she bumped into its chest.

''WHAT, YOU, AGAIN...?''

She then accidentally fell down on her butt on the ground. She fell down on the sidewalk, before its feet. It slowly went down on her, it seemed to be about to prick her again with the tip of its syringe – but luckily for her, just before it could hurt her once more – someone appeared on the sidewalk next to her. It was a man. It was Doctor Ethan Garden. He was there for her. He was there to rescue you. Lauren couldn't believe it. She stayed on the ground for a while, amazed by how heroic Doctor Garden was right now, just for her.

He grabbed the masked man's arm, the one carrying the syringe; he pricked it right into the left side of its neck. It caused a distraction. Doctor Ethan Garden quickly grabbed Lauren from the sidewalk and helped her run back to the medical clinic, where he came from to help her.

"It's totally up to you if you want to stay or leave, but I'm taking you with me for now, that's for sure."

He said while mostly carrying her. They ran back to the clinic.

As they were running, Lauren stayed silent. For a short moment, she turned her head around and looked behind them. The man in the mask with the red crosses was motionless. It was standing there on the sidewalk where it attacked her. It stared at her, falling back to the clinic. It never moved. It didn't want to move.

***

Later, once they were safe, once they were back inside the medical clinic. Lauren and the two boys, Doctor Ethan Garden and the bald man were resting at the entrance room, nearby the secretary's desk. The old secretary wasn't around. Not behind her counter but rather on break it seemed. We could hear a woman that sounded just like her laughing down the hallway.

"So, that was why you didn't want me to go?"

Lauren said, breaking the uncomfortable silence.

"I'm afraid so."

"Yup..."

Doctor Garden said before the bald man interrupted him.

"I don't, I don't get it, why are we safe here and not out there?"

"It can't enter this place."

The bald man continued.

"Um... Okay, what about the other people outside this clinic, AKA the rest of the world?"

"Don't worry about that, it's hard to explain but it can't hurt anyone. It can... It can only hurt *you*. I'm sorry to say that but this is true."

Doctor Garden said to her, revealing her more info on what is really going on.

"Why me? It can only hurt one person and it happens to be me? Why?"

The two men turned to each other. They didn't seem to be sure how to answer her. So, someone else did for them. Director Cameron Ross. He surprised the three sitting in the corner of the room. He revealed himself to them. It seemed as if had been there, looking and listening to them for some time now.

"It can *only* stalk, find, and hurt *you* because you are very unique. You have a really unique ability that not a lot of people have. You can actually sense and detect a rare kind of virus that the media have no idea about. You can even cure special diseases. That's why it is trying to take you down."

"Are you saying that because a few weeks ago I was still working as a nurse? It's not because I was a nurse at some point that I have special abilities or something like that. You all know that right?"

A beat, a silence paused the conversation.

"Right...?"

She kept asking them, trying to make sure she was not crazy. After a few seconds, the director slowly walked closer to the three in the corner.

"I know it's quite complicated to grasp. It all happened so fast for you. But I swear to God. It's all true."

The director kept insisting. She inhaled and exhaled. It was tough.

"And... You three are the only ones who actually know about all this?"

The bald man stood up and softly placed the palm of his right hand on top of her left shoulder.

"Exactly, this clinic is a cover up for us. This is on the surface a typical hospital where normal medical consultations and operations are done but the ones who run this place. Director Ross and us, we are secretly doing something else entirely. We are treating cases that no one else even knows exists. By the way, despite the fact that you didn't listen to us about leaving, I'm actually very happy you're still alive."

After his further explanations, he smiled at her while making his joke. He then removed his palm from her shoulder and offered her to shake hands.

"I never properly introduced myself to you; my name is Doctor Noah Carter. Nice to meet you."

Lauren accepted to shake his hand. They shook hands as he was slowly bringing a smile back on her face.

"And I lied. I'm not gay, at all."

Noah Carter continued while wiggling his eyebrows.

Meanwhile, Doctor Garden noticed how much Noah was quickly able to bring her smile back. He interrupted them and placed himself between the two.

"Alright, we should maybe go back to work now."

"Absolutely..."

Noah responded to Ethan. Almost immediately after the short-lived comedic moment had happened, a new emergency came up. An ambulance came at full speed and stopped outside right in front of the clinic's doors. It caught the attention of the four in the corner inside. The paramedics quickly came out of the ambulance and brought a man on a stretcher inside.

Director Ross and the two doctors instantly ran to the newly arrived patient. Lauren followed the three. At first, she had a lot of trouble seeing the man on the stretcher. She had to make her way closer and closer to the stretcher.

When she finally saw the patient and his identity was revealed to her, she discovered that it was her neighbour: Mr. Samuel Rogers. He was burnt. Most of his face was burnt. He was in a critical situation.

CHAPTER SIX

Back in the emergency room, this time Lauren was not here as a patient, but rather as a witness to someone fighting for his life. Someone she had known for a very long time. She now had to trust those newly met persons to save him. On their way to the emergency room, during their rush in the hallway, Ethan almost immediately noticed something radically important about Mr. Rogers. Despite all the horrible burning he had suffered from, he was also suffering from something else, a different disease not a lot of people had. It was a virus. The kind the four were recently discussing at the entrance of the clinic. It was one of the many rare and supernatural, erotic viruses that this secret brigade of doctors had sworn to cure. Noah and Director Ross both helped pushed the stretcher as Ethan first noticed the presence of this type of virus in Mr. Rogers; meanwhile, Lauren did her best to follow the group.

"His tongue, it's all green. It must be... It must be one of the erotic viruses we are after."

Ethan said in a panic.

"It *could* be. It could also be a fungus. By judging from the look of it, it could be an overgrowth of fungus."

Noah argued.

"No, it's not. It's too much of a coincidence. He was burnt. This man is probably Miss Winkler's neighbour, right?"

Director Ross yelled as he helped to push the stretcher against the doors leading to the emergency room. Once inside, Lauren confirmed Ross's question and theory.

"You would be right Director Ross, this man is my neighbour. This is Rogers. I knew he was in trouble. Why did it take them so long to find him?"

"I only read the quick briefing from the fire department but he was apparently discovered about fifteen minutes ago. He was hidden under a pile of ashes and furniture in his apartment. It's a miracle he only suffered from this little amount of burning."

Director Ross told her, trying to calm her.

"WHAT A BUNCH OF ASSHOLES AND WORTHLESS TRASH? THEY GOT ME OUT OF THERE BUT NOT HIM?"

Lauren screamed. She was furious.

"Well, he's out of there now. And we can still save him, that's what matters now."

Ethan responded to her. While Ross and he took care of Mr. Rogers, Noah turned around, he faced Lauren.

"I'm sorry, young lady, you're going to have to stay behind."

"WHY...?"

"Well, you're not a doctor. You're not even a nurse. You can't help. You need to stay out of the emergency room."

Noah pushed her out of the room; he closed the doors on her and made sure she was going to stay outside.

"But, no, I'm actually a nurse. I was a nurse before I got fired."

She kept talking to him, barking at him through the doors.

"We all know about that here. But, you're no longer a nurse now. You also have an attachment to this patient. Stay out. We're going to take care of him."

He then turned around, he went back to help Ethan and Director Ross.

The three men surrounded Mr. Rogers. They did their best to act as quickly as possible. Her neighbour was lucky in his tragedy. Despite not having been a working a nurse for awhile now, Lauren could easily see from the window she was peaking through that Mr. Rogers was only suffering from minors burning. She could tell it was only first degree burning on his face. Just like Director Ross previously said, this was a miracle, Lauren completely agreed with it after she partially succeeded to calm down from the other side of the doors.

Minutes later, after the two doctors and the director were finally able to calm some of the pain down, one bigger problem remained: The state of Mr. Rogers's tongue. It was still green, a disgusting toxic-looking green. His tongue was bigger and thicker than what a typical tongue should have been.

I've never seen his tongue as large as this.

Lauren thought. It was so big it couldn't stay in his mouth at all. It kept sliding off, oozing smelly, green saliva all over his face and the stretcher. Mr. Rogers was still unconscious.

"This is it. This is *not* fungus. This got to be one of the erotic viruses, the green tongue one."

Ethan announced in the emergency room.

"Alright, alright, it might be that. But, look, we're screwed because we haven't found anyone yet. We still haven't found an immunized person to cure this type of virus. We don't have an immunized woman with us."

Noah complained. He was negative, sure, but he was also pretty realistic. Finding an immunized individual to help cure sick persons of erotic diseases was already extremely rare. Finding an immunized lady or a man willing to go erotic with another man was even rarer.

"No, you're wrong. We found someone. But we, we never tested her before. It's all happening so fast."

Director Ross told the others.

"We have no idea if she's truly immunized to this. We just met her. We still have no idea, sir. If you don't do something now, this man will die. His tongue will get so big he will no longer be able to breathe."

Noah argued.

But, suddenly, as the three men were about to fight each other regarding what they would need to do next, Lauren burst opened the doors. She forced her way back inside the emergency room. The expression on her face had changed. She was calmer and more confident. She was no longer yelling. She was in control of herself.

"Tell me what I need to do, and I'll do it."

The three men were baffled. They didn't know what to do or what to say. They eventually let her in. She gathered around the still unconscious Mr. Rogers with the doctors. His green tongue kept getting dangerously bigger and bigger by the minute.

"It's going to sound weird but you need to kiss him. You need to kiss your neighbour. You have to kiss his tongue in order to stop it from growing any more."

Ethan calmly said to her.

"Well, if you are truly immunized, it will work, if you're not, it will probably only give me a boner."

Noah continued with his snarky attitude.

"Look, Noah, I have absolutely no idea what I am. But, I want to save my friend. Alright, is that good enough for you?"

She responded to him.

"If you want to do it, do it. I believe in you."

Director Ross boosted her up while pushing Noah out of her way. Lauren then slowly walked up to the unconscious Mr. Rogers. She took a frightened look at her neighbour before leaning forward. She closed her eyes and started opening her mouth. She was blushing, a lot. She had no idea she would one day have to kiss her friendly neighbour. Despite him being a good person and all, if this was not to save him, she would have never kissed him. He was a lot older than her, by at least forty years and he wasn't her type.

At first, she only kissed the tip of his green tongue with her lips. She already knew it wasn't enough, she knew she would have to use her tongue as well. Her using her lips was probably to warm herself up to it. After sticking her slimy tongue out of her mouth, she finally made contact with it. The tips of the two tongues were touching each other, dancing with each other. You could already tell it was going to work. The green tongue had progressively stopped growing. It was stabilizing itself.

Lauren then pushed the operation further by opening her mouth very wide and using it as a vacuum to suck on Mr. Rogers's tongue. She started sucking on it as if it was a penis. She sucked on it with her mouth till a ton of saliva kept dripping off, covering his green tongue. This was now pretty clear; Mr. Rogers's tongue had stopped growing bigger.

"Boner: Confirmed."

Noah said behind Lauren.

CHAPTER SEVEN

The next morning, Lauren and the two doctors had a new meeting with their leader, director Ross. This was the aftermath of what had happened last night. Lauren had succeeded in stabilizing the situation of her neighbour, Mr. Rogers. His green tongue had stopped growing, but it was still huge, it still looked like it was covered in fungus. He was still unconscious and he didn't seem to be about to wake up anytime soon. It was useless to say the situation was bad. It could have been a lot worse than that for sure. If the three doctors weren't able to take care of the burning and if Lauren didn't stabilize his tongue, things would have definitely gone south, very fast.

The four were all sitting together in the throne room of Director Ross. Ethan and Noah were placed together, sitting on chairs in front of the big desk, while the director himself was on the other side of it. He was on his throne. Lauren seemed to be the odd one out; she was sitting on a chair at the right edge of the large desk. She seemed a little separated from the group in a pretty unusual way. Perhaps it was because she was the *new* one. She felt part of the group and excluded from it at the same time.

Lauren was no longer wearing her overly revealing and atrocious hospital patient robe. She had recovered her own, normal clothes she was wearing during *the* night everything went down. Finally, she once more wore her thick, warm sweater, her pair of jeans, and her leather boots. Her clothes had been washed and carefully dried off following the intense contact with the dangerous smoke. Her clothes were not the only things she had happily recovered, her cell-phone was another. Speaking of which, her phone was currently sitting on top of the big desk in the throne room. She had it, yes, but she wasn't using or playing with it at the moment. Lauren was in the middle of a conversation with the three men. It had been over a day now since she called her ex-boyfriend and yet, still no answer from him at all. No sign at all. She had forgotten about him. Screw him.

"So, after attentively analyzing and monitoring the state or Mr. Samuel Rogers this morning, I can positively say his situation has been successfully stabilized. It's not good; it's not bad, it's better than nothing. His life is hanging in the balance. He was unconscious since the very moment he was found and brought here. It could have been the shock of the events, the pains of the burning or the erotic virus he is suffering from that caused him to be in this coma."

Director Ross explained to the three.

"Let's talk about this for a minute. What *is* exactly this virus?

Lauren asked.

"It's what we have been studying here for a very long time now. This green tongue virus is one of the many erotic viruses that exist out there. The public mostly doesn't know anything about it. It's all a secret. We are a covering this up. Despite being very dangerous, those erotic viruses are very rare."

Ethan answered.

"If it is so rare, why and how Rogers got it...?"

"For the longest time, those viruses were supposed to be extinct. They disappeared in the mid-eighties, around eighty-four. But now, it all came back. It came back here, in Thunder-Falls and in the area around."

Noah continued.

"And we think this man, this masked man might have something to do with it."

Ethan said.

"Then, why am I so special? Before Rogers arrived at the clinic, you were telling me about special abilities."

She asked.

"Yes, we strongly thought you were one of the people that was immunized to these erotic viruses, we suspected it. But, now, we know. We ran tests and only a woman among a million has that immunization. It's in you. It's genetic. And this immunization grants you the ability to cure sick people that have those viruses. It was revealed to us yesterday when you successfully stopped Mr. Samuel Rogers's tongue from growing. You stopped the infection all by yourself. It's quite remarkable. But, now, you would need to go farther in order to save our patient. You would need to do more."

Doctor Ross explained to her. She slowly cocked her head to the left side. She showed a confused expression on her face.

"What... What do you want me to do then? I kissed the man. I kissed him with my tongue. I kissed him a lot with my tongue too."

"I *vaguely* recalled something like that."

Noah said with his traditional snarky voice. She turned herself around and looked at him to discover he was smiling at her all along. He was basically teasing her, making fun of her a little. At this precise moment, it was pretty obvious Noah had adored what he had seen yesterday when Lauren kissed Mr. Rogers. He might have enjoyed it a little too much. She stared at him with a disgusted expression on her face during a long silent pause.

"What? I remember it, pretty well too."

He said to her while keeping his jokey smile.

"Ignore him."

Ethan then told her in her right ear. Lauren turned back to Director Ross, continuing the discussion they shared before Noah interrupted them.

"Look. I want to save him. I want to save my neighbour. What do I need to do?"

For a second or two, Director Ross turned to his two doctors, made eye contact with them, and then went back to Lauren. He grinned.

"You would need to give him an erection while he is still in his coma. Then, you would have to provide him an ejaculation."

This time, a real, awkward silence broke their discussion in half. A silent beat filled the throne room. Lauren seemed surprised. Her eyes were wide opened, the same thing for her mouth. The two doctors both leaned forward looked at her, stared at her for a long time while remaining silent.

"I know, I know. This is not going to be easy for you, I imagine. But, once the patient would have ejaculated, the erotic virus inside of his metabolism would have become extremely weak, weak enough to get rid of it, weak enough to fully destroy it..."

Director Ross paused for a minute. He stood up, opened one of the many drawers from his desk and pulled something out of it. He took a small, ruby red chest out of the drawer and held it in his hands. He directly showed it to her Lauren.

"... Weak enough so you can pull the virus out of the patient's body using this."

Ross continued. One more silence interrupted the conversation after. It actually took Lauren a couple seconds to get herself together, to close her widely opened mouth and to speak again.

"... So, you basically want me to become a medical prostitute, and hospital whore, right?"

She said.

"No, no, nothing of this nature Miss Winkler, I would rather say: I would like you to become a nurse again, a very special nurse."

Director Ross said to her while opening the small chest in his hands. The content of the chest was ultimately revealed to Lauren. Inside, there was a large syringe, a unique kind of syringe with a cute, ruby red cross on it.

CHAPTER EIGHT

It was barely ten o'clock in the morning, yet, the operation to save Mr. Samuel Rogers's life was about to begin. Lauren slowly opened the door of the patient's bedroom – revealing her brand new outfit as she first saw her unconscious neighbour that day – gone were her old clothes. Lauren was now wearing her new and official nurse uniform. It was radically different from the original blue and white nurse outfit she wore as she was working in the general hospital months ago. No, this one was cooler; Lauren thought it looked way better. This one was mainly mauve white with shining, blood red stripes on the corners of the uniform. This outfit seemed to be forcing Lauren to show a ton of cleavage, a whole lot more cleavage than she ever showed before while wearing her previous clothes (such as her old nurse clothes, her sweater, or her patient robe). The exposed cleavage portion of the uniform was so huge that it extended from her neck to very far on her belly, nearly showing her belly button, but not quite. She had a plain white sport wristband on both of her upper arms; they both showed little red crosses. She wore huge egg white coloured gloves that almost reached up to her elbows. She had a cute, white hat on her head; a medical red cross was shown in front of it as well. On her legs, she had sexy, gray pantyhose and white high-heeled shows that made her an inch taller.

She walked inside the bedroom. She laid her eyes on her sick neighbour as he was still unconscious. His face was covered in bandages. Lauren felt deep sadness as she saw him again in this tragic state. She wanted to help him. As much as she could, that was exactly why she was here. She swallowed the saliva in her mouth and slowly turned around. She looked at Director Ross who was still waiting for her in the hallway. He was holding something for her in his hands. The same small chest he offered her earlier in the throne room. It was still opened, the strange and unique syringe lying inside of it. Lauren and Ross made eye-contact.

"For when you will be towards the end of your *operation,* this will come handy."

Without saying a word, Lauren reached her hands and took the syringe out of the tiny chest. She held it very close to her chest.

"Alright, I'm doing this to save my friend, Rogers. But, let's be real. I have no intention of becoming your nurse. I won't work for you after this. And, also, yes, I'm agreeing to have sex with this patient for medical reasons, but that will be the extent of it. Just to be clear, I won't be having sex with Ethan, Noah, or you. Understood?"

"Good luck..."

He then slowly turned around and walked off.

"And I will close this door during the operation, for privacy."

He shook his head while walking away, disappearing in the hallway. Lauren slowly closed the door, inhaled and exhaled. It was time. She turned around and moved to Mr. Rogers's bed. She placed the syringe on top of a bedside table.

While she had been his neighbour for a very long time, and they were only friends, she was strangely starting to feel something for him. Maybe it was because his life was on the line, but she was starting to feel some emotions for the man. She would have of course never told or admitted this to anyone, but it was true. She was feeling something for him. She had no idea how to begin this intervention; she leaned forward and kissed the middle of his forehead. She liked it. It felt right, it felt nice to her. She moved her head down and kissed him on his lips for the first time since the early test when he urgently arrived at the clinic.

Despite being unconscious and all, his lips felt good to kiss. They were surprisingly not dry at all, they were a little wet. She then kissed him again, and again. She eventually kissed him a fourth time, only touching the surface of his lips with hers. Following the fourth kiss, she then slowly removed the blanket Mr. Rogers had on. She pulled it away from his body and threw it at his feet. She was quite impressed, it was the first time she had ever seen his body. His chest was pretty muscular. She touched it, felt the surface of his chest with her palm. Then, she felt his chest with her delicate finger. Her attention eventually switched to his crotch, she focused on his penis.

At that point, Mr. Rogers was only wearing a pair of pants, jogging. She softly slid her hand down from his chest to his crotch and touched the tip of it. It was completely flaccid. It was soft. As she or, anyone would expect. But, the more she kept the physical presence of her hand on it, the more it got warmer. The more it got harder. The more it got bigger.

Without Lauren expecting or, anticipating it, Mr. Rogers' dick was getting erected. Yes, it was not her imagination. It was definitely not her imagination. The man was now hard. This sudden change of events entirely threw Lauren unprepared and shocked. It immediately encouraged her to go back to his mouth. She kissed him on his lips again, this time, while she was holding his cock. This fifth kiss was completely different from the first fours, this time, they both kissed, not just Lauren kissing him. Lauren started blushing as Mr. Rogers slowly opened his eyes. He was no longer unconscious. He had awakened. He looked at Lauren with comforting and rested expressions in his face. They made eye contact. Lauren had the curious feeling she was caught, that she was literally caught during the act as if she had done something wrong. She was also gradually getting so turned on that she never stopped touching or holding his hard crotch.

''I am so sorry; this is not what you think, Rogers. I'm just saving your life right now.''

She desperately tried telling him, quickly explaining why she was holding his dick while kissing him.

''... I know... I'm sick... Do what you have to do... I always thought you made a great nurse...''

He was barely able to tell her as she was now basically on top of him, making a big effort not to squish him too much.

''So, you really don't mind me having sex with you, then?''

''... If you save me in this process? That would be a good thing I think... If the last thing I do before dying is this, that would have been a great conclusion for my life... I would always say: *yes* to you, Lauren...''

She blushed even more than ever before. She stroked his cock a few times before softly pulling it out of the inside of his jogging pants. This was, of course, the very first time she was seeing his dick, and it was incredibly hard. It was extremely large and erected the first time she had seen it. She slid his pants down and started rubbing her right hand all over it. She was starting to masturbate it. She was masturbating her neighbour.

This thing was already oozing with pre-cum. The fingers of her right hand were sticking together as she kept stroking his dick. Mr. Rogers happily stared at her masturbating his cock for a very long time. He had a pleasant view. He was observing her jerking him off as her big boobs were constantly bouncing up and down as she moved.

A few minutes into the masturbating treatments, one of her large tits accidentally slid out of the inside of her new nurse uniform. Only one of them came out. This boob escaped out of her top due to the constant and aggressive bouncing movement caused by shaking her body during the hand-job.

As soon as Mr. Rogers saw her left tit fully revealed and naked, wildly bouncing out of her uniform, a lot more pre-cum started oozing out of his cock. The view of her gigantically large areolas and of her thick nipple was too big to handle for him. Only a few seconds after the big reveal, Mr. Rogers ultimately ejaculated. He had cummed. He shot his semen all over her face, neck and her big breasts. A lot of it ended up on her fingers as well.

Not too long after his ejaculation, Lauren grabbed the special syringe from the bedside table and pricked the tip of the needle in his sick, green tongue. Just like the director instructed her to do. A disgusting, green fluid came out of his tongue and was stocked inside the syringe.

CHAPTER NINE

The operation seemed to be a success, in a matter of seconds, Mr. Rogers's tongue was visibly turning back to normal. The size of it was getting back to what it was before all this and it was no longer green as well. It was back to pink, a beautiful pink that made Lauren happy to see again. She placed the filled up syringe back on top of the bedside table. After cleaning some of his fresh sperm from her face, she leaned forward toward him. She moved her mouth to his and they kissed again. Not only with their lips this time. She opened her mouth very wide, stuck her long tongue out and softly inserted it inside. Deep in Mr. Rogers' mouth. He accepted the filthy kiss by using his tongue as well. Their tongues danced together. This was Lauren's way to show him her happiness for getting through the 'harsh' medical treatments.

Following the wet kiss, Lauren felt something down there. She felt his junk, hard again. She got up to look and it was true, Mr. Rogers was erect again.

"... Thanks for saving me, Lauren... I'm already feeling a little better... I'm sorry about that, I often get hard again after a first, *daily* ejaculation..."

Lauren looked at him, she looked at his cock. She looked at him, she looked at dick. She blushed more than ever before. She grabbed her already exposed tit and brought it a lot closer to his mouth. She offered her long, stretchy nipple to him.

"It's only me and you here, Rogers. Since you're hard again, we should try to milk some more jizz out of you. Just to make sure we successfully get rid of *all* that green fluid."

She leaned forward again in order to prevent Mr. Rogers from having to get up too much. How considerate of her. She placed her already revealed boob directly in front of his lips. He immediately started sucking on it. He used his own mouth like some sort of vacuum, constantly sipping her stretchy nipple deeper and deeper in the interior of his mouth. He

43

accidentally spilled a ton of saliva all over her breasts and chest. Lauren didn't seem to mind at all.

Once she had thought he had sucked on this particular nipple for enough time now, she pulled her other tit out of the inside of her uniform and showed it to him. She revealed and other areolas and her other nipple in a flash, pushing the one that had already been sucked on aside. Mr. Rogers was forced to make the switch. He started sucking on the other nipple. He did so for a very long time. He sucked on it with passion until Lauren could no longer wait anymore. Until her vagina was dripping wet.

Lauren moved aside, she moved away from Mr. Rogers a little. She slid down her nurse uniform and her underwear. She revealed her naked pussy to her neighbour. Like she thought and felt it was, it was completely dripping wet. She was a horny little girl, and her vagina screamed it.

As she had never had a dick covered in semen without a condom inside of her before, she crawled down on him and cleaned it up a bit. She licked the tip of his glans and the rest of his cock with her tongue to make sure most of the semen was completely gone before the inevitable penetration. Some of his cum had covered his testicles as well; therefore, she had to lick them too. And she did. He had pretty hairy balls so it wasn't easy at all for her to clean everything but she got through it. His long, white testicle hairs seemed very disgusting to her at first, but it was only a phase for her. She had to enjoy it to get through it. She had to enjoy it to clean everything up.

After licking his balls, she inserted his dick inside of her mouth, sucking him off a tiny bit. Simply to make sure it was cleaned as much as possible. Once it was done, Lauren climbed on top of Mr. Rogers again. She made sure not to hurt the old patient too much, not placing all her weight on him.

One, two, three, it was in. Lauren had softly but quickly slid her friend's dick inside of her, inside of her pussy. Despite all the kinky stuff they had done together prior to this moment, they were now finally having sex for real. They were fucking together for real. Mr. Rogers was penetrating her. No, he wasn't doing any of the work, Lauren mostly did everything, but he was still helping push it deeper and deeper.

They were both enjoying the Hell out of it, but since he had already ejaculated once today and that she hadn't, she was definitely the one who was the more in need. She kept blushing as she loudly moaned. She was riding Mr. Rogers. She kept jumping, bouncing up and down, and forcing his cock to dive deeper into her.

Meanwhile, he had found the strength to use his arms again. He touched both of her big, bouncing tits as she was fucking his dick. He caressed her massively large breasts. It was as if he had dreamed of getting them for so long in the past. It was as if he had often spied on them from the corner of his eyes in the building they lived, he probably often fantasized about touching them, feeling them. Lauren was getting out of control, she was moving faster, a lot faster. She kept pushing the tip of his dick deeper into her pussy. She desperately wanted to cum that day. She desperately desired to have an orgasm that day. But, sadly for her, what Mr. Rogers was about to tell her could potentially endanger her chances from this happening at the current moment.

"... I have to cum again... It's about to come out..."

It immediately stroked a chord in her, it brought her back to the tamed Lauren she was. Yes, she desperately wanted to have an orgasm, but she specifically didn't want someone to cum inside of her, especially without a condom. In three seconds, she stood up and quickly removed his cock from inside of her pussy. Just in time.

CHAPTER TEN

On the rooftop of the medical clinic, Lauren stood alone; she appreciated the breath-taking sunset. It was dusk, the day was about to come to a conclusion. She inhaled and exhaled as her beautiful new nurse uniform was passively floating thanks to the gracious wind. Doctor Ethan Garden was actually secretly there, on the rooftop with her, his back leaning against a brick wall.

"I know you're there."

He seemed surprised. Ethan jumped a little when he first heard his name. Her delicate and soft voice that confirmed to him that she knew about his presence here was loud enough to catch him off guard.

"You heard me coming up the stairs?"

"Something like that..."

In addition to still wearing her new nurse uniform, Lauren now wore a dark gray scarf. Naturally, the piece of cloth softly flew in the air with the wind as she slowly turned to Ethan.

"You should be proud, you know? You saved him. If you wouldn't have been here in our clinic if you didn't know about us, if you had not discovered any of this... He wouldn't be here with us as we are speaking. He would be gone."

She stared at him as he spoke to her. When he was done, she looked down at his feet. She seemed very sad.

"Great, I'm happy. I swear."

"'But...?"

"But... While the three of you explained to me many times, over and over again...I still can't wrap my mind on how strangely I helped Rogers. I had no idea people could heal other people with... Sex."

"No, you're wrong. Not people. Not most people. Only a few of them, you being one of them... Never forget that, cherish it instead. You can save lives. You can save many more lives if you stay here with us. Well... If you chose to stay and if this is what you want of course. It's up to you.''

Lauren listened to Ethan with all her attention. After a silent beat installed itself between the two, she turned to her home, Thunder-Falls. She gazed at the town she lived in as it was soon about to go dark.

Without her knowing, the man with the mask was gazing at her, down on the ground. Both Lauren and Ethan had no idea it was there, looking at the rooftop. The man was motionless. It was standing between two trees in the woods nearby. It was as if it was simply waiting there for the sun to fall so it could enjoy the coldness of the night.

***

In his hospital bedroom, Mr. Rogers had just recently waked up from his slumber. He had been deeply sleeping since his exciting and healing time with Lauren earlier that day. He literally just got up. He started to stretch his arms while yawning. Both Director Ross and Noah were in the room with him. They were taking care of him as he was getting up.

''So, how do you feel now, Mr. Rogers? By judging from your look you already seemed to be feeling a lot better.''

The director told him.

''Yeah, as a matter of fact, I feel better now. This morning was... This morning was refreshing. I can't tell you why but I feel different since this morning.''

''Oh really...? I can't understand why lucky motherfucker...''

Noah said super quietly before Director Ross stopped him, stepping in front of him and placing the palm of his hand on his filthy mouth.

''Um, wait, what do you mean?''

Mr. Rogers said in response to Noah, whom he had only barely heard but still kind of understood what he said.

''It's nothing. He said absolutely nothing important. What matters is that you feel better. Let's take your bandages off now. Shall we?''

The director said to the patient while smiling to him, quickly throwing water on the fire that Noah had just partially ignited.

When director Ross was done removing the last bandage off Mr. Rogers's face, Lauren slowly and quietly walked in the corridor. Mr. Rogers's bedroom door was wide opened, simply perfect for her to see the result of the 'operation'. Director Ross and Noah smiled upon seeing the patient's face. Miraculously, all the burning were gone. The skin of his face was completely healed. His tongue was also back to normal. The intervention was a success. In the hallway, Lauren showed half a smile. She seemed happy that the condition of her neighbour had become a lot better and that she was the main factor for it. But, she couldn't stop thinking about what was next for them, for her, for the clinic... What did the future have in store for her? What was next? How was she planning to go about it and to choose which path to take?

"How is it? Doctors, please tell me. How's the infection?"

Mr. Rogers begged them. A split second before he asked Ross and Noah, Lauren had already left the corridor. She was gone. She had disappeared like a shadow.

***

Later, down at the first floor of the clinic near the entrance, Lauren slowly walked in direction of the cafeteria. She was hungry. She hadn't eaten much since the medical intervention that occurred this morning. But before she could get very far, she was stopped by the secretary of the clinic.

"Hold on, hold on, it's for you."

Lauren turned around.

"For me...?"

"You received a call, miss."

How ironic? It was one of the only times of the day that she went down on the first floor and someone had to be calling, asking for her as she was going to get something to eat? And who could it have been? No one knew she was here. No one except her ex...

"Lauren, are you okay?"

She immediately heard as she placed the phone on her ear.

"Yes, yes, I'm okay."

"I received your message."

"Hum okay, it has been a while since I called you."

"I know, I'm sorry. I should have called back earlier. How are you really? I'm coming to get you. I'm going to be there for you starting now."

"What do you mean?"

"Look, Lauren, I was wrong. I was completely wrong. I realized that what I did was horrible. Living without you made me realize how bad I need you in my life. Look, babe, just tell what is the number of your hospital bedroom and I'm coming right away, alright?"

"It's a clinic. Not a hospital."

Her ex-boyfriend then took a few seconds to answer her.

"But this place has bedrooms for patients, right?"

Like a triumphant champion, Lauren hanged up the phone, ending the call. The secretary immediately looked at her with approving eyes as she didn't hide the fact that she was listening to Lauren's phone conversation. They didn't say a single word to each other. Lauren handed the phone back to the woman. In return, the secretary nodded to her. Lauren was off to the cafeteria for good this time.

∗∗*∗*

Toward the end of the day, director Ross went back to his throne room. He was alone when he arrived at his desk and dumped his messenger bag made of leather on it. Accidentally, he threw his bag on top of something that wasn't supposed to be there. Something that wasn't on his desk earlier during the day, it was a letter, or rather a hand-written note.

Director Ross grabbed the edge of it after seeing it under his bag. He slid it off the top of his desk and started reading it. It was actually very short but communicated a ton of things to the director.

I'm staying for now.

CHAPTER ELEVEN

A week later, past seven PM, a young man was sitting comfortably at home while watching porn in his living room. But he wasn't masturbating, not at all. The worst about it was that he seemed very much into it. He seemed interested. But no, he never touched himself, he never pleasured himself. After watching the video for a few minutes, he gave up, he turned it off. Porn was gone.

"No, I can't do this. It's bad."

His name was Hector Edgar. It has roughly been a year now since the last time he'd ever touched himself. No masturbation at all in exactly eleven months, three weeks, two days, and fourteen hours. Masturbation aside, sex was not even an option for him right now. He wasn't a virgin or anything like that; he had sex a few times when he was a little bit younger. He was eighteen years old at the moment, he was soon about to turn nineteen in a few weeks from now. Hector had sex with women of his age before he turned eighteen, during his time as a disobeying, dashing teenager. Make no mistake, Hector was still a teenager, at heart, soul, and at the surface as well.

But, here was the thing: He wanted to grow up. He wanted to have sex with women, a lot of them too. He thought of himself as a widely arousing young man for the ladies. It was not that he was ugly, no, far from it. He was okay looking, he was average. He was normal. And it might have been that he lost himself. He wasn't making any real effort to get laid; he simply thought his natural charms would have been good enough to pick up girls easily. And he was wrong. That's wasn't enough. He had to do more. He had to try. He had to flirt with girls. But, he wasn't ready for it, and it was very apparent. In the meantime, his only options were either paying someone to have sex with or having to pleasure himself. He was broke. He didn't have the money to pay someone; it probably wasn't something he would have been comfortable to do anyway. So, masturbation was a viable solution here.

And this was where the *real* problem was: He was ashamed of the mere concept of masturbating. The reason why: His parents, or rather more specifically his dad. Hector had a very poor sexual education back in the days. He was now suffering from it. He was taught that masturbating was bad, wrong, a sin. It was not like he listened to his dad during all his life, no. He pleasured himself a lot in the past. But, he had stopped masturbating a year ago; he couldn't bring himself to do it after his girlfriend dumped him.

His trouble to jerk off was a combination of many things. He was getting frustrated to live with this issue. Hector went to the bathroom of his apartment to wash his face. He threw cold water in his face to rinse it. He then started to change his clothes. As it was night time and that he had work early in the morning tomorrow, he was about to put on a pajama. It was when he pulled down his pants and slid down his underwear that the really *real* issue was revealed to him.

His lack of will to sexually satisfy himself didn't stop at preventing him from having some fun. No. This entire problem caused his testicles to have grown to a very abnormal size. Instead of having grape size balls, his testicles were now about the size of oranges. And it seemed to be getting worse by the minute. We could see many blue veins all over them, twitching as he slid down his underwear. Sadly for Hector, while his balls were now massively large, his dick was very normal still, seemingly average in term of size and overall appearance. Well, not even the size of his cock was actually under average. Only two inches long, it was fair to say that it was indeed a micropenis. It was so sad to see how big his testicles had gotten. His dick was simply left behind apparently. Hector didn't tell his problem to anyone yet, he was too ashamed. It was getting complicated for him to hide them as well. At that point, he was doing his best to cram them between his legs. Hector simply had no idea why this was happening to him. He had never seen someone else with this problem.

"Fuck it..."

He yelled while staring at his crotch.

A few seconds later, he walked back into his living room. He opened his TV and turned on the porn video he had given up on an earlier. He sat down on his couch to watch it. The video showed a *'step-father'* having sex with his

51

'step-daughter'. The lady had huge tits, exactly what Hector loved and enjoyed the most, exactly what he couldn't have. The man was bald, old, and ugly as fuck.

She was offering the best blow-job he could have ever asked for. The oral performance of the actress was remarkable and messy. Hector didn't take the time to fully put on his pajama as he rushed himself out of the bathroom. His pajama top was on his body, but he was fully naked for the rest. His giant testicles were comfortably sitting on top of the couch. It, of course, caused Hector to not sit too comfortably or properly on it, but at least, his balls were resting on something and not just hanging down in the air. His cock was hard. The porn video was definitely turning him on.

He seemed pretty decided to fight this masturbating block he had. He jerked himself off really fast and intensely. Pretty much the best he could while keeping the size of his penis in mind.

But, something horrible happened to Hector. During the masturbation, his testicles grew bigger again. It grew larger to the point of swallowing his tiny cock in the crack of his balls. Therefore, completely preventing him from masturbating any longer, stealing his dick away from him.

"No, no, no, no, no, NO..."

CHAPTER TWELVE

Inside the cafeteria of the medical clinic of Thunder-Falls, at the dawn of the day, it was way too early. Lauren was enjoying her breakfast. She was still wearing her pajama and her cute pink slippers. She was served her breakfast, scrambled eggs, French toasts, hash browns, and sausages. But, something alertly important was missing, her sweet transfusion of caffeine, It was not there.

She soon realized she wasn't really hungry. She had eaten a little bit of her breakfast, some of her hash browns but that was about it. She was instead very thirsty for a caffeinated beverage. It was not like she didn't ask for it, no, not at all, she did, but she only got water for some obscure reason. Lauren didn't know about it until she sat down at one of the tables in the cafeteria.

Lauren slowly played with one of the many long, roasted sausages in her plate. The one she softly moved around was covered in delicious maple syrup, it was dripping wet. She barely looked at it as she wiggled it around. She seemed lost in her thoughts as a man quickly approached her table and threw a pile of files, a pile of medical documents right next to her cabaret where her food was. Lauren looked up at the man – it was Ethan. He seemed stern while she smiled at him.

''How's your breakfast?''

''Fine, I guess...'' She said while giving a mean stare at her plate. Ethan could easily see that she wasn't enjoying a whole lot.

''What's wrong with it? You don't like hospital food?''

Lauren then started getting pissed off at him, a true contrast to how she originally felt when she saw him crashing at her table. She was glad to see him at first; of course, she hadn't seen anyone from her medical squad in an entire day. It was more than fair for her to be feeling like this, after all, all the other people working in this clinic were allowed and safe to leave the building, not her. She quickly crossed both of her arms together as she confronted Ethan.

"Oh, I like it alright, it's just that when I took the decision to stay here, I didn't really think about the idea of having to eat here all the time. And by the way, speak for yourself. It's not like you are forced to stay here or to eat here all the time, you can go out whenever you want to and go wherever you want to. Look, I'm not mad or anything like that, I can survive with this food. I can deal with the clinic food but here's the problem: I specifically asked for a coffee and the man gave me some plain water instead, how I am supposed to deal with that? It's not even flavored water."

And this was when Ethan revealed something he was hiding behind his back the entire time – a deliciously warm and creamy cup of coffee. Hot steam came out of it as if it was a fireplace. Lauren soon noticed it as he showed it to her, slowly but surely moving closer to her. She stopped having her arms crossed together, her hands were instead stuck to each other as if she was about to pray. As if she was about to pray to Ethan for the cup of coffee. Her eyes were big and rounded. Her mouth was wide opened a little bit of saliva was progressively leaking from it.

"A cup of coffee... Is this for...?"

"You, I brought it just for you, I don't like coffee."

Ethan delicately handed her the coffee. She grabbed it and took a minuscule but a needed sip from it.

"How come you don't drink coffee?"

"I prefer tea."

After a second, and a much bigger sip, she placed down the cup next to her cabaret and continued the conversation with the doctor.

"But I don't get it, how did you know I didn't get a cup of coffee?"

"Nothing special, I saw from a distance that you only had water to go with your meal so I went to get a coffee for you before coming to say hello. I recently arrived at the clinic from home."

He said while sitting on a chair in front of her. Instead of eating with her, he opened some of his medical files to work while sharing a discussion with his new co-worker.

"Home, that sounds nice."

Following the last things she said, Ethan seemed to be hoping to change the subject a little. He began by clearing his throat before speaking again.

"How are you feeling since the recent operation you completed?"

"Well, it was over a week ago now. What about it?"

"You saved a man's life. How does that affect you? I'm not directly talking professionally, but rather emotionally?"

A long silence interrupted their talk. Lauren looked down at her coffee, took a few more sips and avoided to eyed the young doctor too much.

"Since you are a doctor... Can I really tell you everything? Like, are you going to make fun of me if I say something a little strange and personal?"

One more pause slowed their conversation down. Ethan stopped reading his files, placed down the pen he had in his hand and looked at Lauren. He focused on her. This time, he seemed to be taking her a little more seriously. Not that he didn't before, but now, he was laser focused on her and how she might be feeling after everything that had happened.

"Yes, I promise you. You can tell me anything."

"... To be honest with you, before the recent operation, I was not having a whole lot of sexual things happening in my life. My sex life was pretty dormant since I got separated from my ex. And now that I had to do things with my neighbour in order to cure him, I think it kind of changed something in me..."

She said, whispering very quietly.

"How so...?"

He calmly responded to her.

"Doctor Ethan Garden and Nurse Lauren Winkler are both needed at director office. Doctor Ethan Garden and Nurse Lauren Winkler are needed at the director office."

Suddenly, the voice of the secretary through the intercom interrupted Lauren. She was about to speak to Ethan again, possibly revealing new things to him. It seemed as if she was about to tell him something important. Instead, she stood up, turned around and prepared herself to leave cafeteria with her coffee in hands.

Ethan stood up as well, remained motionless for a while with his hands comfortable sitting in the side pockets of his doctor coat. He watched her leave with a sad expression on his face.

Before slowly starting to follow her, he looked down at the tray with the leftovers of her breakfast. He saw the long sausage dripping in maple syrup she kept wiggling around like a dick getting sensually rubbed.

CHAPTER THIRTEEN

Lauren was already entering the director's office when Ethan was barely able to keep up with her. He was running in the hallway, he seemed to be hoping to eventually catch up with her but it never happened, her fast walk was... Well, too fast for him.

Noah and director Ross were both waiting for the two others to come. Director Ross was sitting behind his desk while Noah stood near it. They turned to Lauren as she ran into the office, nearly dropping drops of her warm coffee all over the floor.

"What's up, why did you demanded me so early in the morning?"

"We didn't just summon you, we asked for the other fourth member of the gang as well. Where is he?" Noah asked, not very politely.

He was right tough. Ethan was nowhere to be seen up until now. Lauren had outrun him and left him pretty far in the hallway as she was basically escaping him, moving away from the topic they were talking about. At first, she wanted to confide herself to him but ultimately stopped herself at the very concept of it.

"That's right, did you see him? Were you with him?" Ross asked right after his employee, Noah.

"He was right behind me." Despite the fact that yes, she used their call from the intercom as an escape from the situation she was in earlier, she quickly found herself honestly surprised that Ethan didn't get here sooner. She looked over the shoulder at the door entrance of Ross's office. He was not there. She then slowly stepped back, pushed her head out of the doorway to see where Ethan was in the corridor by herself. In the end, he wasn't too far; he was almost there, only a few feet away from the office of the director of the clinic. Lauren simply looked surprised as Ethan seemed out of breath; he was definitely not able to keep up with her.

"Oh, so you're here?"

"... Yes... You run really fast..."

57

"What do you mean? I only walked... Maybe barely jogged..."

***

Once the pretty nurse helped Ethan crawl into the room, the four members of the secret group working in the shadows of the clinic were reunited on this beautiful morning. Director Ross gave them the usual beginning of the day briefing after explaining to Lauren why this meeting took place a little bit earlier than usual, perhaps around about an hour earlier than usual (hence why the young nurse questioned the old man about it). His answer was clear; it was because he had received some very good news regarding the state of Mr. Rogers, Lauren's ex-neighbour.

"Yes, that's right. From what I heard, the treatments that you gave him, Lauren seemed to be successful on somewhat of a longer term. A few hours after the *operation*, his condition had gotten better. Now, from what he told me over the phone, things keep getting better for him. His tongue is fully back to normal. I will soon have him come by the clinic for a new checkup just to make sure everything is a-okay, but so far, it all seems like very positive news to me."

Lauren immediately jumped into the air, accidentally making her huge tits bounced and flapped all over the place. She was happy to hear all this news. While Ethan and Noah seemed pretty glad as well, they were busier observing her titties moving up and down. Well, not that much for Ethan, he was mostly still busy catching up his breath. No, Noah was definitely the number one pervert in the room that stared at her breasts flapping before his eyes.

"Yes, I'm so happy for Rogers, I knew the operation had been worth it in the end." Lauren said, filled with happiness.

"The operation you conducted worked like a miracle, good job." Ross complimented her.

"I agree with you. The things you did to help this man, wow, it was awesome. Now, I kind of wish I had the same issue was this old dude and that you did the treatments on me too, if you know what I mean." Noah inserted into the conversation.

It almost automatically caused Lauren to stop feeling happy, she stopped jumping up and down, and she stopped smiling. She slowly turned to Noah and gave him a mean glare.

"I don't like your tone. I didn't do it for pleasure. I did it to save him. And Rogers is not just a random man or an old dude. He's my neighbour."

"Or rather *was...* Right...? And, oh, did I forget to tell you? It was actually nice to see you giving the old man the treatments of the operation." Noah shot at her.

"Um, what do you mean? I was alone with Rogers, the door was closed and the blinds were too. You didn't see anything."

"If you want to believe that, go ahead then. But, I didn't need to actually be in the room with you to see what was happening there. I only had to set up a camera in there. But, hey please don't take it too seriously or the wrong way, it was not for my own personal pleasure, it was simply for scientific, educational, and medical purposes only."

"Are you kidding me? Did you really placed a camera in the room?"

But before Lauren could ever get a chance to obtain the information she desired from Noah, their boss, director Ross interrupted them.

"So, I really hope you didn't mind me calling all of you for the morning meeting an hour early. Since I broke the recent news to you, now, let's get to work. We still don't have any new sexual cases to work on, so we'll all have to help the other medical units in different parts of the clinic. Noah, please head to the cardiology department, Ethan, the audiology department."

"Yes, sir..."

Both doctors respectfully said to their boss. Ethan with a little bit less enthusiasm and energy. They both quickly came out of the room while Lauren stayed here. She was furious Noah was escaping; he was getting through her fingers as she hoped to interrogate him concerning what he'd just said.

"Did you set up a camera in the room, Noah? Answer me."

While running, he turned his head to her and smirked.

"What do you mean? I didn't say anything. I don't know what you're talking about."

"Man, you better not have done that or I'll kill you myself, take what you filmed and... Destroy it..." Ethan said to his colleagues as he was barely able to keep up with him, still out of breath.

"Right... I'm sure you will *'destroy'* everything and not keep it to yourself... Sure..."

"Uh, what do you mean?"

And they were gone. Out of sight, out of reach, we could no longer hear them as well. They were now too far.

Lauren then slowly turned around; she turned to the director of the clinic. She changed her anger for Noah into respect and kindness for her boss. It was hard but she did it.

"What about me, boss? What department do I go to?"

"Oh, you'll see. You'll see very soon."

He said in a slow, quiet, and almost creepy but still charming voice.

CHAPTER FOURTEEN

And what the director gave her as task to do was definitely not what she imagined with the creepy and strange tone he had while asking her. No, far from it, Lauren now found herself in the basement of the medical clinic, in the dark basement of this local hospital. While the clinic itself up there felt and always looked like a beautiful haven of well being, the basement automatically seemed like a dungeon to her. A scary dungeon that had nothing to do with the place she had just started to get used to for a little over a week now as the permanent resident that she now was, not only as a patient.

Lauren moved slowly, she ventured into the basement. With each step, she remembered why her boss asked her to come here. While the two doctors from her brigade were both sent to do *real* jobs within the clinic, Lauren was here to find something for the director. She was sent here in the basement to fetch something for him, a navy blue satin box.

She searched for it for a while. It felt as if the basement wasn't visited very often. It was dirty down here and it was dark, making it very confusing to walk around here. Only a couple of lights still worked. During the search, Lauren tried many of the light switches she encountered on her way within the basement. In the end, only about twenty-five percent of the switches had an effect when turned on.

"Hello, anyone down here?" Lauren said while searching. She didn't yell it; she barely spoke it out loud. It was merely a whisper. She was too scared to talk too loud or to make too much noise.

After a quarter of an hour of almost blindly investigating in the dark, Lauren had finally found it. The satin box was hidden in a drawer in a corner at the end of the fourth room she visited, exactly like director Ross told her where it would be. And just like he instructed her, she was forbidden to look into it. It was a direct order from her boss. Was she going to listen to his order? Maybe, maybe not... Well, she clearly had a strong desire to open it but not right now, at least. She was too scared of the darkness surrounding her to open the box at this specific moment. She was willing to open it, but only once she was out of here, out of the basement. She wouldn't see much anyway, keeping in mind how dark it was in here.

But on her way out, she saw something that attracted her and stole her attention, more than anything else she saw in the basement. Even more than the pretty navy blue box she held in her hands. It was a door. A beautiful, tall, and immensely large door made of white oak wood. After observing and contemplating it for several minutes, she tried opening it and, of course, it would not open. She tried looking for a key around but never found one. Why would a key be awkwardly lying around next to a perfectly closed door just like that? She had no idea but this had been the reflex she just had. This was also when she heard something in the back of the room she was in, a sound as if someone had just moved. But she thought she was alone in the basement. Perhaps she was not.

"Who's there?" She yelled, this time not shying away from speaking loud, not whispering like she previously did. After a frighteningly scary silent that lasted an entire minute, Lauren received a call on her cell-phone. The sudden sound of the ringtone scared her to death. She then got a hold of herself and answered the call.

"Lauren, you should come back up to the director's office. Something came up. It's urgent. We got a new..." It was all that Ethan had the time to tell her before the call ended with a ton of loud static noise.

"Ethan? Ethan? Can you hear me? Ethan?" But no, he couldn't hear her. In less than a second, Lauren was once again back alone, in the darkness of the clinic basement. Shortly being on the phone with someone temporally helped her feel better. Not anymore.

***

Now freed from the darkness that surrounded her, Lauren rushed herself in the stairs that lead her back into the clinic. Once back upstairs, she took one short moment to take a look at the small navy blue satin box she held in her hands. Yes, she was in a hurry to get to the director's office but she was also very interested in the box itself. She thought about the idea of opening before joining back with the others as she now walked in one of the many corridors of the clinic.

"Lauren Winkler is demanded at the director's office. Lauren Winkler." The secretary announced through the intercom of the establishment. Lauren didn't pay much attention to the fact that her name was called through the intercom; she, of course, already knew the reason why. She was about to open the box when something much more urgent raced in the hallway right before her. Two E.M.T. ran past her eyes, pushing a stretcher with a man lying on top of it. The man had giant testicles. They were hanging from both sides of the stretcher, flapping and bouncing all over the place as the man was pushed in the corridor. The attention she had for the blue box had completely switched to the man on the stretcher. When the two E.M.T. ran in front of her, the actions of their movements were in slow-motion for a split second. For a split second, she saw the visibly sick man sharing eye-contact with her. Lauren's head first looked down at the tips of his testicles, then she slowly raised her head up in the air until she could see the face of the man. After exchanging looks, the slow-motion trance ended and the two E.M.T. left with the new patient. Soon, the three of them would be completely gone from her sight. As soon as she saw the large testicles, Lauren started feeling hot, warmer, moist, she was already getting wet only seeing the biggest pair of man balls she had ever seen.

"Lauren Winkler is demanded in the emergency room. Lauren Winkler, in the emergency room."

CHAPTER FIFTEEN

"There she is. Finally here..." Noah said while waving his hands in the air.

"It's enough, Noah. Get off her back. She was down in the basement." Ethan quickly struck back at him. The two boys saw her coming from the hallway as she was about to enter the emergency room of the clinic. Lauren had finally joined them. She looked at them, a little at Ethan but mainly at Noah. She stared at him for a while as she moved between the two men.

"I wish she would take care of my basement." Noah continued, pushing his luck, testing the boundaries of Lauren's boundaries.

"What is it? What happened to this man?" The young nurse asked the team.

"We don't know so far. As you can see he just got here. He was found like this, in his apartment." Ethan explained.

"Found? What do you mean?"

"A member of his family found him like this, his mother." Ethan kept explaining. The two E.M.T. had finally left the room. Lauren, Ethan, and Noah were now alone with the patient. He was conscious but silent, he seemed too tired to speak or move much.

"His mom found him? Must have been a shocker." Noah joked.

"His name is Hector Edgar. This is the first time we ever registered such a symptom here. This is definitely not something that could be treated... Let's say... Normally, I don't think the rest of the clinic or the nearest general hospital could do anything for him. That's why the director intercepted the 9-1-1 call from his mother." Ethan explained some more.

The two doctors and the nurse gathered closer around the patient on the stretcher. Lauren was the one that got the closest to him. She delicately grabbed his head and brought her generous chest very close to his eyes.

"Where is the director?" Lauren asked her crew.

"On his way." Noah answered. Lauren was still holding the blue satin box in her hands.

"Hector, how are you feeling?" Lauren quietly and politely asked him.

"Not too bad but you're wrong. My mom was more shocked to catch me fapping as she found me than she was seeing my big balls." He said, joking. He had no energy or almost no energy at all but still, he was able to speak. He was even able to try to be funny. Lauren softly laughed at his joke.

"I don't quite agree with you. I clinically think she might have been more *surprised* to see your.... Things... But don't worry, now that you're here I'm going to take care of you. We'll take care of you."

"Are you a doctor?"

"No, not exactly. I'm a nurse."

"How's a nurse is going to save me? I mean, look at my balls, lady. I think I need a doctor."

"The two other members of my team here, they're doctors. Doctor Garden and Noah are here to help me. But we think you have a very rare type of sexual virus in your body. We simply have to find which one it is."

"And once again, how a nurse is supposed to help me? No offense."

"Well... I'm a special kind of nurse." She said with a gentle and gigantic smile. A smile almost as large as Hector's testicles.

***

Very soon, Lauren pushed the two doctors out of the emergency room. She wanted to be all alone with the recently arrived patient. She smiled while softly pushing the doctors out of the room.

"What are you doing Lauren?" Noah yelled out.

"I'm taking care of this case for now on. I did it once. I can do it again."

"Does that mean you are going to?"

"Yes."

"Can we watch?" Lauren simply nodded *'no'* in response to his question.

"Come on, man, we should let her do her things." Ethan said. It seemed to be hurting him so badly to let her do that again. It seemed to be killing him having to know that she is going to have sex with someone else than him while he never had sex with her. She seemed to be turning him on a lot. She finished pushing them out of the room and closed the big door on them. Before closing the door, she handed the satin box to Ethan without saying a word. He simply accepted it while keeping his eyes on the patient. She then went back to the patient. She stood next to Hector's stretcher and smiled at him.

"You said the two doctors were going to help you. Why did you send them out of the room? I don't understand." Hector asked, stressed out.

"Because we'll need a little privacy."

"Privacy? What for?" She hoped to make him relax a little, she kissed him. It was not a romantic kiss at all. It was an all around kinky, perverted kiss. She opened her mouth very wide and stuck her tongue out of it. Upon realizing what was going on, Hector almost accepted his fate and the situation right away. He opened his mouth as well and invited Lauren to come closer. Soon enough, her tongue was naturally inserted inside of his. Hector didn't share a whole lot of his tongue with her; he was perhaps too shy and surprised to do so. No, *she* did most of the sharing here. After kissing for a few minutes, the patient opened his eyes and was accidentally cut from the real-life erotic dream as he saw the two doctors staring at them through the glass door of the emergency room. He urged her to end this kiss with him.

"Your colleagues. They are watching us. Didn't you say something about a little privacy" Hector asked the nurse. Lauren slowly turned around to see Ethan and Noah perversely starting at her. They were not only looking at her kissing her patient to make him relax, no, no, no. They were literally standing there staring at her huge butt as she was partially lying down on the stretcher with Hector. Her ass was sticking out up in the air in the two doctors' direction. The bottom part of her skirt had been accidentally lifted up as she lied down with the patient, therefore, allowing the doctors to see her partially naked butt, still covered in her bikini style red underwear. After looking at the two men for a while, Lauren slid down her skirt to prevent them from continuing to see her ass; she then stood up and went to the glass door. She moved a large curtain and closed it so the doctors could no longer see inside the room, entirely blocking their view.

CHAPTER SIXTEEN

As Hector's legs were now widely opened and Lauren dove between them, she lifted up his hospital robe to get her first glimpse at her patient's dick. She had seen her testicles a lot recently; they were visible and unveiled to her from to get-go, entirely impossible to be covered under the minuscule hospital gown. The robe was enough to cover his penis though. As she got the clothing fabric out of the way, she was surprised to discover that his cock was about normal, average size, maybe below that, she didn't know, wasn't completely sure. The sexual virus Hector had in him seemed to have contributed to the growth of his balls but sadly did nothing for his dick. His member was not small or tiny by any mean but it had strangely never seemed to grow compared to his balls. While his testicles were the major factor that was turning her on, his dick aroused her as well. Lauren personally enjoyed penises of all sizes, shapes, and colours. And this one was no exception.

"What are you going to do to me?" The patient softly asked as if he was about to faint, probably partly due to his sickness, and partly due to the current situation within the emergency room.

"I'm going to do what I'm here for, siphoning the bad out of you. Siphoning the bad out of your balls." And she wasn't lying, this was her indeed her goal. She started by licking the tip of his glans. Hector had never been circumcised; she had to lick his foreskin first. By the time she got through it, his cock was already hard, he was erect. She then used her right hand to stimulate him some more in hope to get him as hard and sturdy as she desired it. But masturbating his dick wasn't enough, it wasn't enough for her from a medical and personal point of view, she opened her mouth really wide. She inserted his glans inside of her mouth and sucked on it. It was, therefore. the beginning of a clinical blow-job. She kept masturbating him while sucking the Hell out of his dick.

When she was done keeping his cock up and rubbing up during the hand-job, she let go of it to use her hand for something a little different. Both of her hands. She had to use them to grab his majestically large pair of abnormal testicles. She first tried to lift them in the air but she soon understood and realized it was simply an impossible task. After only being able to lift them about one to two inches in the air, she placed them back down on top of the stretcher. She then prepared herself for something a little simpler but just as effective, she sensually rubbed and caressed his balls hoping it would help drain the virus out of him. All this as the blow-job was still in full motion and was getting better, faster, stronger, and crazier by the minute.

"I don't mind it, I don't mind it at all, but is this really going to help?" The nurse never answered the young man. No, she was way too busy. She kept sucking on his cock, making a ton of noise, slurping, moaning... She was definitely into it.

"I need to be honest with you. I need to tell you the truth. There's something I didn't tell the other doctors. They asked about it but I lied to them. They asked me if I've been recently sexually active or if I was plain and simply masturbating on a daily basis. I said yes. I said yes. Yes." She wasn't answering or speaking but she was listening. She listened to all her patient's words. "But it wasn't true. At all... I didn't actually have any sexual relationships in a while. A long while... And I never masturbate. It's true. I never do. I'm scared of it. I refuse. I restrain myself from doing it." He continued, speaking very fast. He was panicked.

Interesting.

She thought. It immediately struck a chord in her. What Hector just said made her think. While she was deeply listening to him and thinking about what he was saying, she never stopped pleasuring him. She wanted him to feel better, sexually and medically. And what the young man just said might be of some major help to her.

Lauren got more aggressive, more brutal. She moved her head up and down as she sucked Hector's dick. It was as if she bounced away from it and was constantly pulled towards it. His cock had turned all slippery; it was covered in her saliva and in his precious pre-cum. The two of them mixed together seemed to be turning in some sort of slime. She also kept rubbing his giant testicles as if her life was depending on it. At some point, she even

68

started squeezing using her palms and her fingers. It didn't hurt him. Not one bit. It actually seemed to be making it feel better. It probably provided some kind of satisfaction and relaxation for the pain he was enduring. Yes, his constantly ever growing balls were hurting him. But not anymore, not as much at least, now that he had Lauren to take care of him, things seemed to be getting better. However, his dick was slowly but surely getting progressively lost between his two large testicles. But luckily for him, she had a way with finding cocks, and this one was inside of her mouth at the moment. And she wasn't going to let it go anytime soon.

A few additional minutes into the blow-job and Hector had reached his limits. He ejaculated inside of Lauren's mouth. He quickly shot all his sperm inside. He moaned and yelled in pleasure. Lauren did the same as well, but she was harder to hear since she was getting her mouth full, her mouth getting filled up more and more. When he was done ejaculating, she pulled his cock out of her mouth and kept all the semen in her mouth unsure if she should swallow or not. She kept this pose for a long time until she finally realized that this whole thing didn't really help. Hector's testicles were still just as big.

***

On the other side of the glass door, Ethan and Noah were still standing there, listening to everything that was happening in the emergency room. They could hear very well but could only see small glimpses of what was going on. The curtain that blocked their view was not fully closed, hence why they could see a little bit in the room. But the two doctors had to fight against one another for it. It wasn't easy. Their fight ended as director Ross finally joined them. He ran towards his two employees. Ethan handed him the blue satin box.

"She is on the other side. She gave me this for you."

CHAPTER SEVENTEEN

The team had retreated. Lauren and the three men were looking at each other in the throne room that basically now mostly served as a meeting lair. It was silent. They didn't know what to do at first.

"You locked yourself in there pretty quick, Lauren. I wish you had maybe waited for me before starting the operation." The director said in a soft but still somewhat comforting voice.

"Why? So you would have been in a position perform the operation?"

"No, not at all, you know it's not the case. I simply wished we could have discussed a plan of attack first."

"You bring up a good point. Where were you exactly?"

"Upstairs, I had my hands full with other patients. I came as soon as possible."

"Well, I'm sorry, I was confident. I thought it would have worked just fine. I thought a good blow-job what was he needed. I mean, it went well the first time I did such an operation last week with my first patient of that kind."

"The blow-job was a great idea. It didn't work but that's okay. We'll think of something else." Ethan said with a sweet and kind voice.

Lauren turned to him, exchanged a smile with him and then turned back to director Ross. She went up to him to be more intimate with the old man.

"Before all this happened, before the new patient came in, you asked me to go down in the basement of the clinic. I found the object you wanted. I handed it to Ethan for you. Was this truly the specific item you asked me to find?" Lauren whispered to the director. He didn't immediately respond to her. He instead turned around, went into the drawer of his desk, grabbed the blue box and showed it to the young nurse.

"Yes, it is."

"What's in the box?" She kept whispering.

"You didn't take a peek?"

"Of course not. I listened to your instructions. So, what's in the box?"

***

Later on during the day, while Ethan and Noah were both brainstorming perverted ideas in hope to cure the new patient, Lauren was charged with another task to complete. After making the two doctors leave the meeting room, director Ross had a word alone with the nurse. He asked her for something dangerous. He personally asked her to go outside where the man in the mask with the red crosses could potentially catch her. He told her there was a wooden cabin outside the clinic, near, behind it. He told her she had to go there and bring him something that was hidden in the cabin. When she would have acquired this second item, he would show her what was in the blue box.

He said what is in the satin box would make sense once I find what was hidden in the cabin. Director Ross said everything would make sense.

Upon arriving near the cabin, Lauren saw a chain that kept the door locked. She looked around for a few seconds, searching for a way to get rid of the chain. She then found a small axe. She took it and used it to slice the chain in half, breaking. She tossed the axe around in the snow. She tried opening the door of the cabin, it didn't work. She then charged and pushed on it with her right shoulder, it worked. The door opened.

Inside, it looked like a normal cabin in the woods. The strange thing was that she had never seen or heard of a cabin behind a clinic or a hospital before. But then she remembered that she lived in Thunder-Falls. A small town that was mostly surrounded by thousands and thousands of trees, the town was surrounded by woods.

But then, the cabin that seemed normal to her turned out to be quite unique as she investigated it. Many posters of beautiful and sexy looking women in bikinis covered the wooden walls of the place. Having those posters in a cabin wasn't abnormal, but having all those here, behind a medical clinic seemed odd to her.

After searching the place for a while, she finally found what she was sent here to find. Another satin box, this time, a crimson red one. She took it and

71

got out of the cabin as soon as possible. When she fast walked out of the cabin and stepped on the cold snow outside, she totally missed something very important. She missed a man that watched her leave the cabin. It was the mask with the red crosses. It patiently watched her leave without moving an inch. Lauren never saw it. Never.

***

Before reaching the main entrance of the clinic, she had to cross a long and huge parking lot the separated the clinic to the cabin. Despite the size of the parking lot, she only needed a few more minutes to get inside the clinic, to be safe from danger.

But just before she reached the entrance, something interrupted her and blocked her way. *Someone.*

It was Lauren's ex-boyfriend.

The one who dumped her, tricked her, and made her lose her job at the general hospital of Thunder-Falls, the place she recently used to work at.

"I've finally found you, Lauren. I've been looking for you for a week."

"You? Here? What are you doing here? I don't want you here. I don't want to see you."

He tried hugging you. She immediately refused. Totally declined. But then, as she fought against his hug, he accidentally made her turn around, the hug was sadly for her still in full motion, he was about to hug her for good.

As he accidentally moved her around, Lauren caught a glimpse of what originally was behind her ex-boyfriend – the man in the mask – it was there, slowly walking toward them. She saw him for the first time in a while. She panicked.

"I want to talk to you. I needed to see you." While she still didn't want to see or talk to him, Lauren didn't want him to get hurt. And she knew her ex couldn't be safe from the man, her ex couldn't see it giving where he looked. That was why she grabbed his hand and brought him inside the clinic.

"Alright come inside, it's cold out. We'll talk." She lied.

CHAPTER EIGHTEEN

In the waiting room of the clinic, the two past lovers stood close to each other in a crowd of people in need of medical help. Lauren made sure her ex-boyfriend was okay. After looking at him, she turned her head to the windows on the wall. She observed the man in the mask still slowly walking toward the entrance of the building. As always, Lauren was the only one who could see it.

"Lauren... Lauren... Lauren...Talk to me... Honey..." Her ex desperately tried to wake her up from this awkward silence as she stared outside. This last word: *'honey'* shook her up. It bothered her. As she kept ignoring her ex, she saw the stalker outside disappearing before her eyes, vanishing into thin air. When it was completely gone, she turned back to her ex.

"Don't call me that. I'm not your honey. I haven't been for a very long time now. What you did was immoral, it's unfixable. Get out of my life."

"But, Lauren I'm sorry but I think it's all fixable. Please let me try to fix things up. I love you. I want to be with you."

"You betrayed me. *You* betrayed me. You got me fired from my dream job. You dumped me as I was *sex-caming* with you. Screw you." She had then already forgotten why she just saved him. Wait a minute? She didn't. From what she remembered based on what director Ross told her, the man in the mask can only hurt Lauren. Or the persons like her who can heal people through sexual ways.

"But, honey..."

"STOP CALLING ME THAT." She yelled at him, furious as she spun around, attempting the get the Hell away from him.

"But, come on, I always called you that. It isn't about to change now." He insisted.

"Consider changing a ton of things right now. Stop bothering Lauren and leave at this second." Ethan said with a demanding tone. He was there.

73

He was here for her. They both turned to the young doctor, they both looked surprised.

"Ethan..."

"Who are you? The new boyfriend?"

"Not quite, just her new colleague. Lauren has work to do. She work here as a nurse. If you don't have any health issues, you don't belong here." She was impressed by him. She blushed a lot. It took her ex-boyfriend a little while to leave but he did, Ethan's glare helped. He saved the day.

***

Within an empty patient bedroom, Ethan strongly grabbed Lauren from the ground and delicately pushed her against a wall. The two kissed. At first, with their lips only. But very quickly with their tongues as well. Lauren couldn't help it. It had been a full week since her first patient and she had nothing up until now, any sex, not even some simple self-pleasure. And she had been recently turned on by Ethan. He was a good looking man. Ethan licked her neck, her throat. It was evident he was hot for her. He wanted her. Next to them, the crimson red box could be seen sitting on furniture.

"We can't do this. It's not right. I can't."

"Why? I don't understand, I thought..." He replied.

"Yes, I find you very attractive, but I can't have sex with you, I made myself a promise."

"What promise?"

"As a nurse, I only and strictly want to have sex with my patients. No one else. With Rogers, it was so exciting. Doing with patients is better and it is even better if I remain exclusive to them."

"I see, so... We cannot do anything then?"

"Let's rather say we can do everything except full-on sex."

"Which means?"

Lauren got down on her knees. She unzipped Ethan's pants and pulled his erect dick out of it. She immediately started licking, and then sucking on it. It was not her first blow-job of the day so she was alright, she was warmed up. This one was going to be better than the first one of the day. Ethan moaned as she pushed the palm of his hands against the wall in front of him. Lauren pulled her breasts out of her nurse uniform and inserted his twitching cock between her tits. She started performing a titty-job for him. She occasionally licked the tip of his glans with her tongue during, teasing him; it caused the doctor to shoot a constant flow of pre-cum out of his penis, covering her boobs. After a solid five minutes of titty-fucking, Ethan seemed to want to change things up a little. If Lauren wasn't willing to have full-on sex with him, perhaps he could a little something for her. He placed her on a patient's bed and widely opened her legs. He crawled between them, went under her skirt, pushes her underwear aside and used her tongue on her. He licked her clitoris, the entrance of her pussy and the interior of it.

This was definitely something Lauren wasn't used to. *A giver.* Someone that was actually willing to give back to her.

In only a few minutes only, Ethan's oral talents seemed to be enough to make the young nurse reach her orgasm. She had her orgasm. She moaned and tried her best to not to scream too loud. When she was done feeling her orgasm and that she had to stop Ethan from continuing to lick her (yeah, despite her being done, *he* wasn't done, he was more than willing to keep licking her, over and over again). When Lauren was forced to pierce her claws in his back to make him stop, he stood up and finished himself up. He masturbated and ejaculated all over her beautiful breasts.

***

Meanwhile, Lauren's ex-boyfriend was spying on them, looking at them through the opening of the door. He was fapping in the hallway of the clinic, often looking around to make sure no one saw him. He eventually ejaculated, not too long after Ethan did. While no one physically saw him during this afternoon, he forgot to pay attention to the many cameras of the establishment. He had been filmed without him knowing.

CHAPTER NINETEEN

Lauren and Ethan were out of breath. They went to the throne room to meet back with the rest of the medical unit. This was what they hoped to do at least. Director Ross and Noah were nowhere to be found. They called their names but they never responded. Through a decent search for them, Ethan ended up finding something he never thought he would lay his eyes on – a monitor in a corner of the throne room – playing footage of the operation Lauren conducted with her neighbour. In the background behind the young doctor, the nurse heard parts of the audio of the footage, but Ethan didn't want her to see that. Not now at least. He quickly turned the monitor off, spun around and covered the screen with his body as if it was going to change something. No, she had already seen some of it.

"What was that?" She asked.

"Nothing, they're not here. We should go check downstairs in the ER."

***

They rushed themselves to the emergency room where the new patient, Hector was brought back to. Director Ross and Noah were there with the patient. Upon arriving there, Lauren swung at Noah and pushed him right in the face. She didn't say anything to him. She paused for a moment and then turned to the director. He seemed scared for his life but instead of being attacked by her, she kindly handed him the crimson red box from the cabin. This was when he revealed to her that he was keeping the blue box with him as well. The two were finally together at last. The old man placed both boxes on a medical table near the patient's bed.

"You are going to tell me what are in those two boxes and why you asked me to gather them for you." She barked at him.

"I won't tell you, I'll show you instead." He then opened both boxes. An object was sitting in each box. They were two parts that when combined

76

together, it would make a complete object, a tool, a medical one. The director grabbed the two pieces and connected with one another.

Click.

It was whole. The tool was a *stethoscope.* A special one, it had a beautiful and glowing amethyst color to it. It was made of real gemstones. The director handed it to her.

"A stethoscope? This one looks very pretty but I don't get it, we have plenty of those, normal ones all over the clinic. While this one right here looks nice, why did I needed to find the pieces to make this one?"

"This stethoscope is unique. Just like you, it has supernatural abilities. This stethoscope can help detect the problems with the special patients we are treating. Remember earlier today, you attempted something with Hector, it didn't work. It didn't work because the blow-job you performed wasn't the correct fetish to realize for the virus he has. *This* will tell us what fetish is needed with this patient."

A beat, after thinking and observing the tool for a while, Lauren finally decided to take the stethoscope. She walked to Hector and started using the object on him, testing it against his chest. She closed her eyes as she was trying to read him.

A few minutes into the reading, she suddenly opened her eyes. She had just learned something.

"What is it?" Ethan asked.

"I can treat him. I know how. But, not here. It cannot happen here."

***

Lauren brought Hector alone with her. She brought him in a large hospital bathroom. She rolled him in on a stretcher all by herself. Hector was awake, he could barely move due to his current condition but he still tried. Lauren rolled him very close to a bathtub. The tub was completely empty and dry. She slid the man off the top of the stretcher; place him down in the bathtub. He actually helped her out during this process, he mostly bounced around on the stretcher with his giant testicles but that had the effect to contribute to what Lauren indented to do. In a few seconds, Hector was lying down on his back in the tub; his big balls filled the rest of it.

Lauren stood in front of her patient. She got undressed before his eyes. She removed her official nurse outfit, let it fall at her feet and she put on something entirely different. She put on a slim, two-piece, autumn red bikini. Hector gazed at her with wide opened eyes. Pretty quickly, his dick got erect and could finally be seen through the separation of his testicles. He was hard. Harder than he had ever been today and for a very long time, it was also the first time his eyes had been laid on Lauren's nearly naked body. She had been wearing her nurse outfit with him prior to this moment. She stretched her arms, passed them behind her head, smiled, and winked to her patient. She was getting ready.

***

"What are you going to do? What did you hear with the strange stethoscope?" Hector asked, worried.

"Your fetish. I heard it." She responded. Lauren was now in the bathtub with her patient. Talk about getting personal and intimate. She chose one of his gigantic testicles, the right one. She climbed on top of the partially hairy thing and started jumping up and down, bouncing up and down on it. She was riding his ball, attempting to fuck it as Hector's cock was throbbing at her left.

***

This was a deeply buried and forgotten fetish for Hector but it was real. It was legitimate. Hector had a fetish for women riding him, not exactly limited to riding his penis but riding him in general. And it that case as he now had giant testicles, it was perfect for him. This was his fetish. He now knew that Lauren saw and discovered it through the use of the weird stethoscope she used on him.

***

Lauren kept bouncing up and down on Hector's right ball. He seemed fully into it. She did as well. She pulled the bottom part of her bikini down and removed it. She made her vagina naked, visible, and accessible to Hector for the very first time. Once again, she kept riding his right testicle, bouncing over it, rubbing her naked pussy all over it. Lauren also accidentally, physically entered in direct contact with Hector's continuously throbbing member. His glans rubbed against her left shoulder and she started caressing with her hands from now on.

Things turned unusual as she felt a second throbbing, phallic, physical entity growing larger and larger within her. She felt a dick penetrating her pussy as she was riding his giant testicle.

CHAPTER TWENTY

Lauren looked down to make sure what she felt was actually real, and it was. She was now getting fucked by a second erect penis that was at this precise moment growing on top of Hector's testicle before her eyes. She kept riding it, bouncing up and down, enjoying it more with each movement. She moaned and never stopped rubbing the original, main, and real cock her patient had.

Soon enough, a third penis grew on Hector's body. This one grew on his other giant testicle, the left one. This fitted perfectly. Lauren had two hands so having two twitching members to play around with was a plus (not mentioning the other very important third cock that was drilling up her wet pussy as she was sitting on the gigantic testicle). She started masturbating both dicks. She rubbed them with the palm of her hands and softly squeezed them with her delicate medic fingers.

This was a three-way action going on between only two people.

To Hector and Lauren's surprise, he had grown a giant pair of balls as well as two additional dicks in less than forty-eight hours.

"What's happening? What's wrong with me?"

"Don't worry, I'm here, the operation has just begun." She said as she also removed the chest part of her bikini and threw it out of the bathtub.

She leaned forward, lowered the chest part of her body in order to bring her face a lot closer to the most recently grown cock on Hector's body, the one on his left testicle. She widely opened her mouth and started sucking this same dick. She was still masturbating his original penis and she was of course still riding the rock hard member that grew on the ball on the right.

She sucked on his extremely erect cock for a very long time. For ten minutes straight, Lauren blow-jobbed this specific member till it shot a tremendous amount of hot, steaming semen all over the interior of her mouth. After she felt that he was done cumming inside of her mouth, she softly pulled his dick out, swallowed most of the sperm, and was about to get ready to observe a radically shocking event.

As the jizz slid in her throat, the newly grown dick she had just sucked slowly disappeared before her eyes – it tranquilly shrank till it was fully gone – or rather most of it, only the glans of the member was still visible on his left testicle. The rest had shrunk down to the point of having being pulled back inside the interior, inside the core of the left ball. She couldn't believe her eyes. As some of the semen in her mouth hadn't been completely swallowed, it softly slid out and covered parts of her lips as she was observing the recent event in awe. Her mouth remaining wide opened for a long while.

Meanwhile, she was quickly snapped out of this distraction as she felt the other recently grown dick getting deeper and deeper into her vagina. She'd almost forgotten about this one. Same for Hector's original member, her right hand was still around the patient's real cock. She went back to rub it, to hand-job it after snapping out of the distraction. When this sexual operation had gone a little too *intense* for her to handle, Hector's second dick accidentally slid out of Lauren's pussy during very deep and fast-paced penetrations. *This* was the wrong time for it to happen. His cock accidentally slipped out of her pussy right after having just starting to feel the warm pre-cum flowing inside of her. As soon as his penis was pushed out of her vaginal hole, Hector ejaculated once more. He came all over her perfectly slim belly.

At the exact same moment, receiving the multiple cum-shots on her belly unfortunately caused the nurse to squeeze the patient's original penis uncomfortably hard during the masturbation. This brutal and intense stroking of the hand unleashed a ton of sperm; it made him cum a third time. Lauren received most of the cum-shots coming out of his original cock on her beautifully sweaty breasts.

***

Nearly an hour after Hector's three cocks have first ejaculated, Lauren found herself bathing in a tub fully filled with her patient's sperm. Her patient was also sharing the semen bath with her.

Miraculously, Hector's last remaining extra dick that grew off his right testicle was mostly gone, same thing that previously happened to the other one. The tip of the glans was still visible on the side of the hairy ball. But, even more miraculous was that his pair of testicles had shrunk down in size, going back to what they were before. Going back to what they normally were.

The patient had been cured by Lauren.

"How did you do it?" Hector quietly asked while comfortably and passively bathing in the tub filled of warm sperm.

"I know how your body developed this sex virus. The stethoscope told me. It's because..." He stared at her, almost scared to know the truth. The tension was real. "... It's because you... Were not masturbating... Enough... Or at all for that matter..."

"I got sick and all this because I wasn't fapping?"

"Right."

"But, I was taught my whole life that masturbating was wrong and dangerous for someone."

"That way of thinking is definitely wrong. Masturbation is important and viral. Especially if you can't get sex on a normal basis. Masturbate yourself. Save yourself." She said as she slowly swam toward her patient in the bathtub, right between his wide opened legs. She delicately grabbed his now very soft and flaccid dick and softly started masturbating it again while looking at him, smiling to him. "Trust me. I'm a nurse. Keep masturbating on a daily basis. For me. For you. Okay?"

"Okay..."

***

Not too long after her operation with Hector and after teaching him to masturbate more often in his private time for his health's sake, the patient was escorted out of the bathroom. Ethan had come into the room and took Hector back to his personal bedroom to rest a little following the treatments. After taking care of him, Ethan went back into the bathroom to see if Lauren needed any help getting out of the tub. She was still bathing in Hector's hot semen. She seemed to be enjoying it a lot. She smiled and blushed while bathing. Ethan stood next to the tub and took a look at her.

"Are you ready to get out?"

"Not quite just yet..."

***

Sometime after bathing in her patient's jizz, Lauren got out of there and went to see Noah again. The last time she saw him, she punched him right in the face after learning about what he did, after learning that he truly had filmed her as she was treating her first patient in the clinic, her neighbour, Mr. Rogers.

As she was still fresh from her warm, steaming sperm bath, she entered the office where Noah was working in, still wearing a thin and short towel. This was the only thing she wore at that particular time. Noah was simply doing some paperwork at a desk as she came by. Lauren quietly entered the room; she made her presence known to him by knocking at the already opened door of the room. It immediately caught his attention; he raised and turned his head to her. He seemed to be getting turned on as soon as he realized she was almost naked, only wearing the towel. He also seemed to notice that she was still covered in semen.

"Noah... I'm not done with you just yet..."

***

"I saw a gate down in the basement. A strange gate."

Lauren said to director Ross in a hallway later on after visiting Noah. She was still only wearing the towel, still a little covered in semen.

"What is there a gate in the basement of the clinic, director?" She continued asking him. He looked at her. He listened to her. He was soon about to answer her...

***

The gate within the basement Lauren was talking about. The one she saw.

83

On the other side, there was a room; the man with the mask. It looked at itself in a large mirror. It removed its mask to reveal the tablet it showed to Lauren over a year ago.

On the tablet, the video Lauren filmed of herself, the one in which she undressed herself for her ex-boyfriend. The one she got fired from the general hospital for was currently playing on the device.

CHAPTER TWENTY-ONE

At a public park during the day, Matthew was jogging like he did every morning. Winter was over now. Spring was here, it was sunny and warm out. All the snow was gone. He only had to go to work at around ten AM but it didn't prevent him from getting up very early. He worked at a community college as a mathematics teacher. It was barely eight o'clock but he was already out in his sport clothes, wearing a gray t-shirt and a pair of black gym shorts. He of course wore running shoes as he ran his way in the park.

Despite being early in the morning, Matthew met a lot of people on his way during his jobbing in town. Not a whole lot of men tough, he encountered many more ladies than gentlemen. Or was that really the truth? Was it actually a fact? Perhaps Matthew had a stronger desire for noticing and seeing the women. This might had blocked his view on the males that was in the park as well. Perhaps he only had eyes for the females.

Matthew didn't live alone. He was not single, not fully at least. He had a girlfriend. They were a couple that took things pretty easy and casual between each other. It had been the case for a while, for nearly as long as he could remember. He pretty much always cheated on his girlfriend. And she always did the same as well. They didn't really love each other, well, not totally at least. Matthew would never admit it, and he was too scared to. Or he could had been a little too stupid to realize it.

No, the two were together more for practical, logistic, and convenient reasons. He was fine with her cheating on him and she was fine with him cheating on her. That was it. He had barely told her *'goodbye'* as he left house to go do his jogging. He briefly took the time to tell her about him leaving the house this morning before work. He thought that it would be short, so he would soon be back anyway, no need to make an exposé about it. His girlfriend was no longer asleep, no, she was still in bed but she was awake. She was drinking coffee in bed. A cup of coffee he'd personally brought her in bed. Now, that he took the time to do that for her before leaving. She quickly thanked him and that was it. They seemed more like friends.

Matthew thought about all the gloriously beautiful women around him in the park. All of them looked better than his girlfriend in his personal opinion. He saw a nice-looking blonde, a tall brunette, and a skinny redhead.

The blonde was sitting on a wooden bench, looking at Matthew as he jogged by. She stared at him, gazed at his beauty and manliness. Was that real? It could have been his imagination, but he had the feeling to be watched by the blonde. He liked it. He almost didn't care if it was real or not, he had the feeling to be looked at by her, therefore, he dug it.

He ran past her. He slowed down a little as he got closer to her. He didn't fully turn his head to her, he kind of looked at her in the corner of his eyes but that was about it. He didn't want her to think he was desperate.

Matthew preferred women being all over him than the contrary. He was already enough all over ladies as it was, that was alright for him. He then kept jogging, picked up his pace and reached the same speed he had before seeing the blonde girl looking at him. As he sped up, he thought about the woman sitting on the bench that he just passed by. He felt a twitching in his crotch.

That was right.

Matthew was getting a boner. He was getting pretty hard too. He felt like he couldn't control it. He looked around and then thought that no one was watching him jogged anymore, he quickly grabbed his crotch to scratch his balls. The real reason behind this wasn't really to scratch his testicles to appease some kind of tinkling down there, not quite; it was rather to correctly position his cock. It had recently changed its pose as it got bigger and harder, making it a little uncomfortable for him. But, now that was better. It felt better for him.

As he turned his back around, he was surprised to see one of the other ladies he first saw when he arrived in the park actually looking at him. This female was the redhead one. She was not sitting on a bench, she running, she was jobbing, just like him. She ran a lot faster than him. She was ahead. She kept an eye on him as they competed in their race; she had the time to see him grabbing his nuts (or rather tactically re-positioning his dick).

The woman with the red hair had big boobs. They bounced around, up and down as she ran.

As soon as Matthew saw her running, looking at him, smiling to him, it triggered his cock, it grew bigger again. The boner wasn't about to end. But, it was different this time around. Instead of giving Matthew a comfortable and satisfying sensation, it actually hurt him. His dick hurt and he didn't know why. He felt and heard his own underwear stretch, shred as his penis pierced through it.

He stopped running, therefore, admitting the defeat with the redhead woman. She smirked at him as she realized that she had won. She also seemed to have noticed that he stared at her breasts for a short moment. It probably made her very happy. She then kept running and left. Matthew was out of breath. He took a look inside his shorts to confirm he'd really pierced through his underwear. It was the case. It kept hurting him really bad. He had no idea why. But, then, he was surprised again – this time by a lady walking her dog – she was the pretty brunette he saw when he entered the park.

She perhaps saw Matthew looked into his shorts, maybe, he was not sure. He realized that she had even bigger tits than the blonde and the redhead. It accidentally caused him to pierce more than his underwear; he went through his shorts with this erect cock this time. His throbbing member was fully revealed to anyone looking at him in the park. The brunette saw it. Her dog barked at Matthew. Something wasn't right. Matthew's cock grew up to an abnormal size, up to three feet long; it crashed on the ground before the brunette's feet. It hurt him again. She seemed scared at first but then she got closer to him, she felt worried for the man.

"Oh my God, mister, are you alright?"

CHAPTER TWENTY-TWO

A little over a week had passed since the young nurse had emerged into the throne room of her boss, still covered in her patient's sperm, only wearing a thin towel. Without any new patient to take care of, Lauren had more than seven days to prepare for what was about to come. Back when she questioned director Ross about the underground gate, she had finally gotten the answers she was hoping for. Or rather, some of them.

"Use the syringe. Use the stethoscope. Use both of them at the same time."

"Could you give me an hand? I'm pretty sure the two holes are a little too far away from each other for me to reach the both of them at the same time. I kind of have short arms." Lauren responded to the director as they stood in front of the large gate within the basement of the clinic.

"Are you sure you want to go through with this?" The old man asked.

"I've been thinking about it for a week, now... Yes... I want to know what's on the other side. It must be something pretty huge since you're not willing to tell me anything about it."

"It's better not tell you much for now. You have to see it by yourself. There, hand me the syringe and I'll do the hole on my side." She handed it to him. He inserted it in the hole on the wall near his left. After watching him do it, she turned to her right and did the same with the stethoscope she was still holding in her hand. They then both turned the two medical tools at around the same time, looking at each other while doing so to make sure they were more or less synchronized. The two objects were keys. This was the only way to open this gate. And it did. The gate slowly started opening before their eyes. When it was all opened, the two stared into a dark corridor on the other side. Lauren then turned to him.

"Since you've told me how to open the gate, you can have your reward, director. You are free to keep the video Noah filmed, if you want to... Just please don't let *him* have it. Okay?" She told him.

88

"No, thank you. I've already deleted everything that was filmed from when you took care of your patient. I took everything Noah had as well and got rid of it. I was very disappointed he did this. I'll make sure it never happen again or Noah will have to leave our clinic." He responded to her. She seemed surprised, happy, and grateful. She tried thanking him but ultimately wasn't able to do it. She stared at him, she looked down and then turned back to the dark corridor. She grabbed her cellphone out of one of the pockets of her white, medical coat, activated the flash-light on it and then started moving forward. Director Ross followed her.

***

Once in the dusty hallway, the two walked for a few feet till they couldn't see the entrance of the gate anymore it was so dark in here. While at first, the flashlight was enough, it became apparent that they needed something more. Ross took out his cellphone as well and activated the flash-light as well. The more they walked in the corridor, the more it got colder and colder.It had become freezing here. The two could see their cold breathes when they tried speaking to one another, they ultimately never did during the beginning of their exploration of this place.

Soon enough, they started noticing a few medical tools on the walls of the hallway. Just like they "keys" that was used to open the gate behind them, many syringes, stereoscopes, and other objects were pinned to the walls. After continuing to walk and to obsessive the tools, the two began to hear something down the corridor – a whisper. A lady seemed to be whispering down the hallway. Lauren and Ross then slowly moved in direction of the voice.

It brought them to a room at the end of the corridor. The door was half-opened. Before Ross even had the time to go in first in order to protect the lady with him, the lady that was with him went in there running. Lauren charged, pushed the door and entered the room. Ross followed her. This was when Lauren discovered that this room was actually one for patients. It was a standard room for patient care but that was left abandoned. No one was here.

A large mirror a sink underneath it was featured against a wall. The two explored the room.

"The basement of the clinic had many rooms like this one that was previously used in the past for patients that were deemed too dangerous to be kept in the actual clinic. This was a long time ago. Before my time." Ross explained his young nurse. Lauren went up to the mirror and the skink. She discovered a tablet *in* the sink where a little bit of water constantly dripped down from the tap on top of it.

"What is this more modern device doing here in this old, abandoned place?" She asked out loud. But she then immediately recognized it as she touched it. It was the same tablet she saw during her nightmarish encounter with the man in the mask. Lauren turned it on and the video of her masturbating in the hospital she was fired from automatically started playing. It grabbed her attention.

"That's it. It's the same. What is it doing here?" She asked.

Behind her.

Ross looked at her ominously.

"I brought her to you." He said out loud. Lauren turned around, still carrying the tablet in her hands.

Surprise.

The man in the mask with the red crosses was here, in the room with them. It closed the door behind itself. It directly stared at the young nurse.

CHAPTER TWENTY-THREE

Surprised by the sudden appearance of the stranger, Lauren spun around, grabbed a crowbar she found near the sink in the room. She pointed it at the man with the mask. It didn't even react to the recent armament of the lady. It only kind of stood there at the edge of the room, watching her.

"Back off. Stay away from me. What is this, Ross? You opened the gate and brought me here just so you could offer me to him?" She yelled out while quickly moving her head from right to left, from the stranger to the director.

"*It* doesn't want to hurt you. And you're the one that opened the gate, I simply did what you told me to do – explain me how to get here." The stranger silently and slowly stepped closer to Lauren, she barely saw or realized that it had moved, but it did.

"But, you knew he would be here. Why did you do it? Why did you betray me?" She kept yelling. The stranger then walked closer to her, each of its movements seemed to be carefully calculated and it never made any sound while moving in the room. Its arms were down, resting beside its hips, barely moving. There were no apparent threat here but Lauren was scared to death. The menace was showcased and amplified exclusively throughout the stranger's steps. The man eventually stopped its walk right in front of the tip of the crowbar the young nurse was pointing at it. Its chest was only about three inches away from the weapon. After staring at each other for while, the stranger suddenly raised its right arm for the first time since it had gotten in the room with them. Oddly enough, it didn't move its arm with the intention to hurt Lauren or anyone but rather to place its fingertips on the bottom part of the mask it was wearing.

Lauren observed in awe and terror as director Ross remained as far as possible from the mask wearer. The old man didn't seemed to be looking or waiting for an opportunity to escape, but he definitely stayed on guard. The stranger got an old of its mask and slowly started removing it. Each single second mattered for Lauren. She had no idea what was about to go down but she remained calm, stood near the broken mirror in the room and paid close attention to what the man's movements. But to her surprise, it wasn't a man underneath the mask, but rather a woman, an old lady. Not any woman but one Lauren had seen before, often, kind of recently. The person under the mask was the secretary from the clinic. Lauren only had a few encounters with this old, ugly lady, she mostly kept hearing her stern voice over the intercom every day since she had arrived at the clinic but that was about it.

"The secretary? Really?" Lauren said, purely disappointed.

"I've been dying to reveal myself to you for a very long time now." The no longer as strange stranger said victoriously, she seemed relieved to pull her mask away.

"I don't get it, you were the one that stalked me from the beginning? That doesn't make any sense. The director and the others all told me you couldn't get inside the clinic, but you were always there. Always. I saw you come into work every morning."

"Can we go now? Now that she knows, we've got to move forward with our tactic." Ross said, nearly interrupting his employee.

"Not so fast, Ross. I want you to see something else before you leave." The secretary ordered while blocking him the way to the exit of the room. "You two, follow me." The old woman continued. She brought them both to another room, one adjacent to the room for patients in ruin they were just in. In only a few seconds, the three stepped into a different bedroom with only one bed at the center of the room. The secretary invited the two inside, this was when they discovered the body of Lauren's ex-boyfriend, lying down on the bed. His skin was all gray. He was dehydrated, almost fully drained out of his strength. He looked older.

"Oh my God, is he alright? What happened to him?" Lauren rushed herself to him, she knelt down at the bed and place her palms on his chest. Even Ross seemed extremely surprised by this, he didn't exactly seemed to be knowing what to do, he simply stood there at the entrance of the room for now. "Is he still alive? I can barely feel his heart... What happened?" Lauren screamed at the secretary as she turned her head to her.

"I've had sex with him." The ugly secretary said in a cold, controlled voice after pausing and being a little silent for a while. Lauren was shocked. Her eyes were wide opened, same for her mouth. She was broken. "Lots of sex... With your ex-boyfriend..." The secretary continued.

"You mean... You raped him?" Lauren asked.

"No, nothing like that. He asked for it. You know, you shouldn't be too worried about his current state. Remember what he did? Remember what he did to you? You simply behaved as a good, lovely girlfriend and organized a nice sexy live-video for him and look what he did. He betrayed you, He got you fired from the hospital. He even probably cheated on you during your relationship. A lot. That's why I tracked you down and showed you the video when I *met* you at your apartment. It was to make you remember. So, don't feel bad for him. He deserved what happened to him."

"You say you didn't raped him, right? You say that he asked you for sex. So, tell me, how did you managed to get asked by my ex for sex with your fucking ugly face?" Lauren slowly and directly said to her. It generated a long, uncomfortable silence in the middle of their discussion.

"Wait, a second. What is the name of your ex, again? I totally forgot about it. You keep calling me 'ex' over and over again. Does he even have a name?"

"Clayton."

"Whatever... Who cares...?"

"Tell me how you had sex with him."

"... I'll show you." The secretary said after waiting a bit to answer her. She then moved closer to the young man, delicately pushed Lauren aside, and placed the palm of her right hand on the ex's chest. A few seconds after closing her eyes, the secretary started draining more energy out of him, it caused him to look even worse than before, grayer, more dehydrated, skinnier, less lively, older. But on the other side – the secretary was changing – she was becoming younger, turned more radiant, losing fats, her skin looked better. When she was done with the young man, she slowly spun around, turned to Lauren and Ross.

The secretary was now an entirely different woman. She looked a lot younger, late twenties or early thirties. Her pale but pink-ish skin illuminated the dark room from its beauty. Her hazel eyes pierced through the shadows and soon made Lauren freeze in place with the eye-contact. Her long brown hair flew with the wind in the air as she spun around, shining. While the secretary was an old, hunchback cavewoman a minute ago, she was now a tall brunette with beautiful shapes to her. She revealed herself to be a pretty thick woman, she had a large, constantly bouncing butt, huge, rounded hips, and giant tits. Her breasts had grew to an enormous thirty-six L size.

CHAPTER TWENTY-FOUR

Emergency! Emergency! Lauren's cellphone rung at the most inconvenient time. She took it out of the pocket her white coat and read what the notification was all about. Director Ross did the same behind her.

"A new patient." She said, concerned but pissed off for this sudden interruption.

"We have to go." Ross declared.

"But are we going to do? Just leave Clayton, dying on the bed?"

"No, no, we can take him with us..."

"Don't even think about that, he'll be dead before you can bring him upstairs." The secretary argued.

"What do you suggest then? Let me remind you that you're the one responsible for this. If he dies, *you're* the murderer." Lauren asked with a stern tone.

"But he won't. It had never been my intention. He simply needed to suffer for what he did to you." The secretary turned around, climbed on the bed, crawled between the opened legs of the sick man, grabbed his cock and started to play with it, masturbating it. Not too long after, she continued her sexual operations by sucking on it, performing an impressively beautiful blow-job right before our eyes. As the blow-job continued, the man kept getting harder and harder till he was erect. And when he was, his heart started beating stronger again, his respiration went back to normal, he was slowly getting back to what he was before. When she was done licking the top of his glans, she turned around and looked up at Lauren.

"You see? He is alive. Now... May I come upstairs to help you guys with his new patient?"

"No thanks..."

***

95

Lauren ran at full speed in one of the hallways of the clinic, director Ross followed behind and had a lot of trouble keeping up with her. The young nurse reached the entrance of the emergency room, she unlocked the doors using her key and entered. She tried passing between her two partners, Ethan and Noah.

"Lauren? Where were you? We tried telling you, we've been sending you messages since almost half an hour now." Ethan told her while blocking her the way to the new patient.

"Yeah, you were not responding at all... Same thing for the director. Did you see him?" Noah continued with all the questions.

"Out of my way you two, I would like to see the patient." And the two finally moved out of her way. The nurse approached the patient's stretcher, or at least she tried, but despite getting passed the two doctors, she wasn't really getting any closer to the patient, not closer to him, she was instead getting closer to his member. The sick man and his stretcher were both at the far end of the emergency room, about ten feet away from her. But as Lauren successfully pushed the two doctors out of her way and moved forward, she found herself almost running into something that was standing right in front her, something that she'd never seen in the room before the two men were pushed out of her sight. While the new patient was still ten feet away from her, his "injured" cock only ten inches away from the tip of her nose. Right in her face. The patient had a circumcised penis. His exposed glans could almost reach her cute cheeks, the hole in his dick could had easily been filled with her nose. She could smell the erotic and manly perfumes of his giant-sized package.

Yes, this new patient had a ten feet long cock and Lauren thought this was nothing normal, even considering all the other weird stuff she'd seen lately with her new job.

"His name is Matthew." Ethan calmly said to her, attempting to start feeding her a couple information after the discovery of his very apparent symptom.

"We tried telling you what was going on so you wouldn't be *too* shocked when you see it, but you pushed us out of your way. Hasty little girl..." Noah whispered in her right ear.

"What happened to this man?" She asked as she circled around his large glans, walked beside his long cock till she had reached the man that owned this thing. The patient was still unconscious as she first laid her eyes on him.

"His penis supposedly started growing to this abnormal size during a morning jogging in the park. Three women came with him, brought him here." Ethan kept feeding her information while reading statistics from a pad he held in his hands.

"This one reminds me of the last patient we got a week ago. The man with the growing testicles." Director Ross said as she entered the emergency room, finally catching up with Lauren and her race to get here. She took a look at the director as he entered the room, joining the other members of this group, she then shifted her eyes back on Matthew – when she turned back to him – he had awoken, he was conscious.

"Help... Help me, ma'am... Please, it hurts..." Matthew murmured to her, barely able to speak. Lauren jumped out of fear when she first saw that he was conscious again.

"My name is Lauren Winkler, I'm a nurse here, Matthew. Not a typical nurse but one that specializes in strange, sexual, phenomena just like the one you seems to be having right now."

"Did you ever see a case as bad as mine?" It seemed like she wanted to say "yes" but wanted to say "no" because this was radically worst than the last patient she had, as if things truly kept worse and worse each time. While she kept looking at Matthew, exchanging looks, the secretary appeared behind the group in the hallway of the clinic. She observed the situation, sporting a smile on her face.

CHAPTER TWENTY-FIVE

Not even an hour after their initial meeting, Matthew and Lauren were getting ready for the emergency operation. Ethan, Noah, and director Ross all stayed out of the ER, not being allowed to come inside just like the other times Lauren took care of a patient in need.

Inside, the young nursed had placed Matthew under sedation, he'd gotten a little too agitated for to handle. He tried getting up, therefore, accidentally moving his giant-sized cock all over the place, this couldn't be happening, he could had destroyed the whole place. Lauren made him sleep and now she had to find a way to take care of this guy. Two weeks again, she had cured her neighbour, Mr. Rogers, a week ago, she had solved the medical issue with the man with the very large testicles. But now things seemed a little different for Lauren, she didn't know where to start with Matthew. His cock was ten feet long, she couldn't have sex with such a dick, that was she thought upon investigating this thing.

How am I supposed to fuck this penis?

As Matthew was deep asleep, she slowly walked beside his long, straight dick, caressed the side of it, examined how the skin of his monster was harder than any other cock skin she'd ever touched before. For a short moment, she knelt down very close to it. Smelled it while crawling further and further till she'd reached his massively large glans. Once at the front of it, she observed with attention the hole in his glans for the first time, it was of course very dark in there, extremely narrow, she couldn't see much. But while it was narrow, the interior was large enough so she could probably reach her hand and most of her arm down there. The anticipation and the want to do or rather try something a little weird like that was building, getting bigger with every second that passed in the emergency room.

To begin with this strange idea, she used both of her hands to open, stretch the opening hole of his glans as much as possible. It ultimately gave her a better view at the interior of his giant cock very quickly, she also used a powerful lamp that operated behind her, directly pointing at the glans.

Just when the young nurse was about to get a better view at the interior, hopefully trying to see if there was something wrong inside, something that could had indicated her what could had been the origins of the problem – someone made her lose her momentum, making her jump a little as well – this person was the secretary of the clinic.

Lauren quickly turned to her after jumping out of fright, she immediately saw the secretary to her right as she placed down one of her hands on her shoulder. While jumping, Lauren accidentally pushed both of her hands a lot deeper into the interior of the giant cock, therefore, trapping, jamming her arms in there. She didn't noticed that at first.

"Lauren." The secretary told her while softly grabbing her shoulder, involuntary making her jump.

"Secretary?"

"I do have a name you know? And by the way, I'm not even a real secretary, I never was, it was all a facade. Remember?"

"What are you then?"

"A nurse. Just like you. But instead of being a young, rookie nurse like you are, you could say that I'm some kind of veteran. It's almost as if old-school was meeting new-school right now." She said, chuckling.

"I see... What's your name?"

"Tracy... Tracy Castle." Right before Lauren's eyes, the veteran nurse ripped her clothes off, entirely removing her "secretary" outfit, therefore, revealing her true clothes she was wearing underneath, her very own nurse uniform. The one she wore departed a lot from the one Lauren had, her outfit seemed more like a doctor one rather than a nurse uniform. Perhaps it could had been an honor reserved for more veteran nurses out there. Only perhaps. She wore a very long white doctor coat, a beige shirt underneath with most of the buttons unbuttoned, allowing anyone willing to look, her massively large cleavage. She, of course, also wore a bra under the shirt, a black one. She had a dark blue ultra mini skirt, gray stockings, and silver sexy high-heeled shoes.

"Alright..." Lauren's attention then switched back to her current situation after attentively observing Tracy's "transformation". She finally realized that both of her arms were now completely stuck in the hole in the glans. "What are you doing here? I told the guys that I was supposed to be alone in here during the emergency operation... Oh, crap... I think I just got stuck inside... Thanks for making me jumped and distracting me, by the way..." The young nurse continued telling the more mature one.

"Good question. I came in here to see if you needed any help with the patient. Do you need any help with the patient? Or with anything else really?"

"Nope..." Obviously lying to her. Tracy then moved around, circled around the massively big cock, raised her right leg in the air so she could sit down on top of the dick, her crotch sitting right before the beginning of the glans.

It truly felt as if she was riding, mounting Matthew's giant penis.

"Are you sure?" Tracy told Lauren. But then, before waiting or asking any more for her permission to help her, the veteran nurse used her hands to enlarged, widened the opening hole of the glans, successfully freeing from this sticky problem.

But another problem came along when Lauren's arms came out of inside of his cock, both of her arms were covered in sticky, warm, highly smelly semen. Probably "expired" or just simply old sperm that was produced a long time ago by Matthew but that remained inside for some obscure reasons.

CHAPTER TWENTY-SIX

"Come on, let me help you..." The veteran nurse said to the younger one with a soft passion, whispering in her ear as she still rode Matthew's genital.

She smells so great, it's crazy... It's like vanilla...

Lauren thought. After smelling Tracy for the first time, it invited her into an entirely different type of relationship she had ever been part of it. She then decided to accept the situation, to accept her fate. She had been imprisoned and hunted down by her since the moment she got back home, back to her apartment when the man with the mask manifested itself to her. It was as if her life had been stolen away from her, but she also realized something had changed, evolved. Back when Tracy was still hidden behind the mask, Lauren felt lonely, victimized, weak, but now that the veteran nurse was in the open, she was with someone else. She had a shot at having a female friend through this new and intense lifestyle. A minute or two of smelling her perfume brought Lauren closer to Tracy, they almost hugged each other. The older nurse kept riding the giant cock while the younger one hopped on top of the hard glans. Their pussies were now next to each other, about to rub against one another. The same thing for their breasts, with a little push, the two pair of tits would likely meet and feel each other. While Lauren had huge boobs, Tracy's were still a lot bigger, they almost completely surrounded Lauren's as they got closer. Inches by inches... Lauren finally gave in, the pleasurable perfume seemed to be a little too much for her and her face softly fell down in in her neck, her nose resting on her perfectly smooth skin. She blushed, losing herself in this unplanned moment of pure happiness for her. She'd almost forget all her troubles, all the terrifying times Tracy gave her, almost forget she had a new patient to take care of today as her crotch caressed his member. Lauren's face didn't stay inside the veteran nurse forever as she soon moved up to her face. Her right cheek rubbed against her left one. Their eyes were closed but they still found each other lips.

They kissed. For only a short moment. Barely a second. But they had kissed.

"I've been waiting for a new Nocturne Nurse for so long..." Tracy murmured to Lauren.

"Another *Nocturne Nurse?* What is that? What do you mean?"

"You don't know? Unique nurses that can heal sick people of sexual magical diseases such as what we are sitting on right now. You know? Such as all the recent patients you had."

"That's how it's called?"

"They never told you the proper term? Ross never gave you more explanation than that?"

"I guess... Not..." Things seemed to be happening a little too fast around her, Tracy noticed it. She looked at her in a sentimental and caring way, caressed one of her shoulders, smiled to her, trying to cheer her up.

"Come on now, let's cure this patient. Shall we?" Lauren looked up to what could potentially one day become her new mentor. What she just said successfully cheered her up.

"But how?" Tracy slid on Matthew's cock, slid closer to Lauren. They're pussies finally met, collided against one another, clitoris to clitoris. They're massively large breasts softly hit into each other as well.

"You'll see." The veteran nurse grabbed the opportunity to kiss Lauren again, this time with using a tongue. A much longer and more intense wet kiss, their tongues danced together, using their mouths as dance floors, switching location every two seconds or so. Lauren was, of course, getting into it very much, she was the first one to remove her some of her clothes and to pull her big tits out in the wild. Tracy took a long look at her own naked breasts, grabbed them, massaged them, and then eventually licked her right nipple. Lauren blushed some more, moaned as the experienced nurse licked her left nipple.

Soon enough, it was Tracy's turn to do the same with her breasts, she removed her white coat and her blouse, pulled her tits out of her bra, revealing them to Lauren. She observed for a flash second before starting touching them, caressing, licking them as well, devouring both of her thick nipples.

"I think we're both getting kind of wet... I think you're ready to help me treat this guy..." Tracy told her as she jumped off the giant cock, the two ladies changed their positions as they were getting ready to do this operation for Matthew. Lauren was now the only one that stayed on top of the dick, still mounting it, she however changed her position so she could have a better view of the other nurse on the floor. Lauren lied down on her chest on the giant-sized member while Tracy sat on the ground just in front of the massively big glans. She sat on the floor in a tremendously sexy squat pose that made her wet pussy extremely visible as both her ultra mini skirt and her underwear stretched to the point of exposing everything, accidentally hiding absolutely nothing, revealing the genital under. As Lauren was watching, she slowly but straight up entered her right arm through the hole in Matthew's glans. She was very careful with all of her movements, taking her time so she wouldn't hurt the man despite him sleeping at the moment. On the surface, she was fucking his cock using her arm, but this was honestly not what she was doing here, she was actually rather performing a very complicated situation that had for meaning to save his life. She'd seen this kind of sign before, for her, that meant that his life was on the line.

CHAPTER TWENTY-SEVEN

Following a long and thorough operation, Tracy had finally gotten her fingers on the problem in the emergency room. Her right hand and arm probably had stayed inside of Matthew's penis for at least fifteen minutes or so, she looked for something very particular in it, and she might have found it – she took it out – a heart. A tiny, grayish white heart that kept pumping at the center of her right palm after she entirely taken out of her hand and arm from the interior of the cock. It was no normal heart, this one had a penis hanging down the bottom of it, bouncing all over the place as Tracy held it. Lauren seemed horrified, traumatized to see what she had just taken out of the patient's sexual member.

"What is this??" Lauren asked in pure confusion.

"It's a heart..."

"Yeah, I gathered and understood that part already but why was this inside my patient's cock?"

"You've never seen one before?"

"Nope..."

"This... Is... What happens when someone with a magical sexual disease like the other people you treated before in the past wait too long... Never realize they're sick. Most men think it's fun to magically have their cock grow to a large and abnormal size like this but when it gets to that point, it's soon over..."

"What do you mean? Was it too late?" Lauren yelled, turned back to the still unconscious, seeing if he was still alive.

"Oh, no, no, no, don't worry, we were right on time." Tracy immediately did her best to reassure her, telling Lauren the truth. The young nurse still checked on Matthew herself just to be sure. She checked on his heart, he was still there, with them. Alive. When Lauren was done breathing, she turned back to the older nurse and discovered that she was sucking on the little heart's dick, performing a nice blow-job.

104

"What are you doing, Tracy?"

The veteran nurse kept serious eye-contact with the younger one as the blow-job continued, it took her about five minutes to complete this task. When she was done, the heart squirted a decent amount of semen out of its little cock, filled up Tracy's mouth. When the testicles of the heart had fully been emptied, its dick and the vital organ itself started decaying.

It was over for it.

As the quality nurse she was, Tracy calmly placed the dead heart down on a medical table next to her as she swallowed the fresh cum in her mouth. She took the time to show everything she had inside her mouth before swallowing anything, showed everything to Lauren.

"When taken out, the heart has to be emptied. It's a normal procedure. Don't worry. We've saved this patient. We need to leave let him rest now. His cock should turn back to a more "normal" size in a few days or so."

***

Just like she said to Lauren, they let Matthew alone to rest in the emergency room for a little while before eventually moving him to his own personal bedroom within the clinic. The two nurses came out of the ER and entered the hallway, slowly walking together. But something was off here. First of all, director Ross, Ethan, and Noah were not here, they were supposed to be waiting while the operation was going on.

"Hey, where's everybody?" Lauren asked, looking around, starting to move faster, running into the hallway. Tracy remained silent, stayed behind the young nurse wherever she went in the clinic. Ever stranger than her colleges not being present, nobody seemed to be in the building at the moment. Lauren rushed herself to the entrance of the clinic and still saw nobody inside. Nobody inside but she did catch someone outside, still on the perimeter of the clinic, in the parking lot. She saw a car quickly leaving the parking of the clinic. She could see three men inside the car but couldn't identify them properly. Lauren feared the worst, she thought it was the men in her medical team, why were they leaving just like that? She tried running outside, screaming the names of her co-workers, but it was too late.

105

Outside, she observed the car leaving with pain. Tracy followed her, stood behind, placed one hand on her shoulder in hope to show support for her in a way.

"Why did they leave? I'm pretty sure it was them. It seemed to be the case." Lauren sadly said.

"This is wrong. It feels so strange. Something's off."

"I wonder where they went."

"Um... I might have an idea..."

***

Not even half an hour later, the two nurses arrived in a different location of Thunder-Falls using Tracy's car.

Seven-thirty-eight, apartment four on Shadow Heart street.

The place where everything began.

At first glance, they saw no one there, no trace of Lauren's three co-workers or anyone else. The two nurses got out of the car and started investigating the area. As expected, the building was burnt, it was impossible to live there. The entire place had to be redone. At least half the building had been totally burnt, starting with Mr. Rogers' apartment. Which reminded her that she was originally told the entire place had burned. It was false. The two nurses entered and climbed up the stairs, walking very slowly, making sure they wouldn't hurt themselves, stepping on the floor or steps.

Once the nurses reached Mr. Rogers' ex apartment, Lauren seemed to recognize the place despite having been through Hell, through tons of burning changes. Seeing this apartment without its normal or usual occupant was like seeing a ghost to her.

CHAPTER TWENTY-EIGHT

"**S**o, where are they? Where are they?" Lauren asked the veteran nurse as she investigated Mr. Rogers's burnt apartment. "Ethan, Noah, director Ross..." She kept yelling their names in hope they would hear her and get their attention. In her corner of the place, Tracy tried to look by herself for a trace of the two doctors and the director. No one was there. The young nurse quickly got tired of this. Everything seemed to be getting worse and worse, it was another wrong thing after the other. She turned around, stopped looking for the guys, charged at Tracy's back, placed one hand on top of her right shoulder. "Alright, *Tracy,* now tell me where the are. You brought me back here. You told me they would be here."

"It might appear that they are not..." The mature nurse finally responded.

"Oh, you think? You know, I'm starting to feel a little weird with you. Here. My old apartment building. This is the place we met each other, the first time we *saw* each other, it was here. You attacked me here. But then, you bring me here and the others are no where to be found."

"I didn't attack you. I've already told you. I'm sorry how *intense* the actions I've done might have been but I would have never hurt you. Both you and your friends."

"Well, then, let's talk about what everything happened exactly. *The* night you cornered me in this building, you pricked a syringe in my neck."

"Correct."

"But why?"

"Alright, here's the honest truth. I did it so I could get you out of the building without you trying to keep running away from me. I wanted to protect you from the fire. I got you out just in time."

"... You did? So, that means... You weren't responsible for the fire? At all?"

"I'm afraid not... When you were safe, I let you lying in the grass far from the building. I then went back inside for your neighbor, Mr. Rogers, but I unfortunately couldn't save him, I couldn't get to him, the fire was too strong already. I tried... I was relieved to learn that the firefighters were able to save him before the fire had spread to him in the room of his apartment."

"But, if you hadn't anything to do with the fire, who did it then?"

"I have no clue..."

"But, what about when I tried running away from the clinic the first day I spent there? The stranger in the mask, *you* assaulted me again as I tried to escape."

"Remember how I was acting as the secretary of the clinic? I saw you leave the first day, I abandoned my desk after you left. Once again, I had no intention of hurting you, my desire was to prevent you from leaving the clinic *too* soon... I thought your medical qualities would have been massively important to the special need patients that we received next."

"So, you have an explanation for everything, huh? How about when director Ross asked me to go outside in the wooden cabin behind the clinic? It seemed as if you were just about to hurt Clayton. What would you had done to him if I didn't bring him inside?" During her intense and punching words, Tracy stepped forward, slowly walked closer and closer to Lauren. She moved toward her until she could surround her with her right arm, circle her body, almost hug the young nurse. Lauren was too scared to do anything, she barely moved as Tracy somberly swallowed her with her arms. The mature nurse mostly looked down on the burnt floor, her face mostly hidden in dark shadows except for her lips. She frowned.

"Nothing... I swear to God... I would have done nothing to him... I simply wanted him to stay away from you, hurting him was *never* my intention... Sometimes when I put on my costume and the mask, I change a little, it's like a different persona of mine..."

"Well, can we talk about this *persona* of yours as you are calling it? Why the costume? Why the mask? What are you trying to project with those?"

"It goes way back. When I first started my career as a young nurse like you, years ago. It no longer matters now but it was something my very own hospital director made me do, things that I was forced to wear during work." Tracy cried as she confessed to Lauren. Her tears pierced through the shadows as they brightly shimmered. Seeing this, the young nurse caught

Tracy as she was falling over her, held her in place, hugged and kept her on her feet.

"I see... That's fine if you don't want to talk about it just yet... But I had another question... Director Ross explained to me that you couldn't enter the clinic by yourself for some obscure reason. You were obviously able to, what was the whole deal with that?"

"I have no idea. It was a lie. He probably started believing himself after a while. Our goal was to keep where you could help people the most. Come on... We need to find the others now, okay?"

"Yes. We will." She murmured to Tracy before kissing her. Their first kiss since they had left the medical facility. The mature nurse kissed her back, fully accepted the invitation.

CHAPTER TWENTY-NINE

With absolutely no life sign in Mr. Rogers's apartment, the two ladies decided to search the rest of the building which ultimately eventually lead them to Lauren's old place. They both arrived in her past bedroom, most of it was surprisingly intact say for the ceiling which had been burnt to the point of having degraded to black and dark red colors. Down on the floor, Lauren's messy bed invited Tracy to sit on the left side of it for some reason.

"No sign of anyone here as well... Guess nobody came back here in the end..." The veteran nurse said, giving up, she felt much more fragile as a person especially after what had happened in Mr. Rogers's apartment. This was when Lauren stepped closer to her and placed one hand on her right knee.

"Stop blaming yourself, it isn't about you, the guys unexpectedly left the clinic, we tried looking for them, and you thought they were in. It could have been the case.

"You are so nice to me. I don't deserve it. I'm so fucked up... All the fucked up things I've done... To you, and other people..." Tracy kept murmuring, on the verge of crying.

"I think I get it now. You knew that my ex-boyfriend treated me like shit despite me not seeing anything. Honestly, I would have probably gone back to him if it wasn't for you, for your intervention. You helped me get away from this lame life. I have you to thank you for that." Lauren then slid down, sat on Tracy's muscular and thick thighs, basically rode the veteran nurse, circled her arms around her. She kissed Tracy, lips to lips at first, then very quickly with her tongue. It entered inside the mature woman's mouth, it took her a while to understand what was happening but she of course accepted it. She responded with her tongue, sliding it in Lauren's mouth, tasting, eating, devouring the many sugary flavors of the young lady. The latter then removed the white coat Tracy wore, opened her beige blouse by unbuttoning it, revealing her cleavage. It didn't take her a lot of time to get

110

rid of the bra she wore which was getting in the way of accessing her breasts. As soon as the the bra was out of the equation and threw away on the floor, Lauren grabbed Tracy's big boobs, softly pushed them against one another, making them look larger, perfectly positioned as she rubbed her fingers on her towering nipples. Caressing her tits was only the beginning as Lauren dove in the crack of her breasts to taste them, starting with her left nipple. Two minutes into it, she had had plenty of time to lick both of her areolas, sucking on her two nipples.

Despite the intense and satisfying sensations that the mature nurse continuously kept receiving, she seemed to be interested in what Lauren had to offer as well. Still while the young lady sat on her laps, riding her, Tracy undressed her new friend, getting access to her naked breasts that had never been covered by any bra during this day so far. This was her turn to grab, caress, lick, and suck. And she did, enjoying it for at least as twice the time that she had her titties sucked.

Lauren moaned a lot as she had her nipples devoured, all those extremely erotic feelings accidentally caused her to lose her balance. She fell forward against Tracy's chest, causing the mature nurse to fall backward onto the bed. The two grown up women screamed like little girls as they both fell down together in the middle of the bed. The two blushed as Lauren was now fully on top of her, exchanging looks. They broke the silence by kissing each other using their tongues again. In even less time than it took them to undress their tops, Tracy fully removed the rest of Lauren's clothes. The young nurse spread her legs as the mature one entered between them, sliding her long tongue all over her already wet clitoris. Lauren had to firmly and strongly squeeze the pillows under her head as Tracy was eating her pussy. As if it wasn't enough to go crazy, to moan, to scream in pure pleasure, the experienced lady started using her fingers. She fingered her pussy while swinging her tongue all over her clitoris. Lauren then quickly grabbed Tracy's hair, pulled it a little during the intensity of their sexy moment.

Without Lauren even noticing, the mature nurse was about to use an object as sex-toy while she was still circling her slutty tongue around her clitoris. While not noticing the new presence of this still unknown object at first, she eventually felt it rubbing along her leg at some point. The young woman briefly opened her eye for a second or two just to see what it was all about. The object was Lauren's special stethoscope, Tracy had recently taken it out of her nurse outfit when she undressed her. In a flash, the mature lady used the stethoscope on its owner, pointed the heartbeat reading end of it on her clitoris, re-purposing it as an awkward but very interesting sex-toy for Lauren. Tracy used the reading end to softly rub her clitoris, the sterile cold steel of it siding with her to amplify strange, erotic sensations. She kept licking her pussy during this process, eating the interior of her vagina. Lauren pulled Tracy's hair a lot harder as she kept moaning louder and ultimately reached her orgasm. This sudden orgasm caused Lauren to squirt for the first time in her life, shooting her sensual fluid right in the mature nurse's face.

"Oh my God, did you just squirt on my forehead?"

"I squirted? Really? This is my first time ever!" Before Tracy could clean the thick liquid from her face, someone pushed the half-opened door of the bedroom. It was director Ross, he was alone, wait, no, he wasn't, Ethan walked and entered the room, following his boss. The two girls quickly turned their heads around and looked at them as they showed their faces.

"The guys!" Lauren screamed, desperately trying to cover her naked breasts.

"So, where were you? We've been looking for you for a while." Tracy calmly said, not giving a flying fuck that she was mostly naked in front of the two men.

"You shouldn't have come here..." Ross pitifully said to them. Ethan then suddenly placed one arm around the director's neck, holding him in place, making him his prisoner.

"I don't agree at all. I'm happy you're both here, ladies. I'm the *one* who set this building on fire, *not* Tracy. I wanted the end your life, Lauren before you become a Nocturne Nurse. I now realize that it was all a mistake, I'm relived you survived the incident, glad *she* saved you. And now, I'll have two Nocturne Nurses for myself for the price of one."

CHAPTER THIRTY

Lauren jumped out of the bed, still covering her titties using her arms while Tracy kept her distance from Ethan.

"You're the one who set my place on fire? Explain yourself." The young nurse angrily said to the handsome doctor.

"Yes I did, but that's okay now... Everybody is fine. You and your neighbor are both alive."

"But you want to get rid of Nocturne Nurses? Why?" Tracy asked, supporting her nurse friend.

"No, it's no longer the case, it was a mistake, I have a new idea now. Secretly, I previously wanted to push Nocturne Nurses away from this town so *we,* the doctors of the clinic found a real way to cure our patients. You know? Without cheating using your abilities. But it all changed when I met you, Lauren... According to our researches, less than ten women with your biology could be in our country as we are speaking. It's alright a miracle you two are here in this minuscule town. Starting today, I'll become the new director of the clinic and will use you two for reproduction. The solution to all our problems is right before our eyes. Come on, girls, please agree with me, what if we mass produce immune and healing people like you are, together?"

"Wait, hold on, that *we mass produce* children with who? You?" Tracy asked, confused.

"Yes..." The beautiful-looking doctor quietly responded. The mature nurse started laughing right after he finished saying "yes".

"Well then, let me tell you that, you are one motherfucking crazy lunatic..." Tracy followed after laughing, however, Lauren quickly interrupted her.

"I think that's a good idea. I'm okay with that. I completely agree with you, Ethan. Let's start right away."

"Are you sure?" The young doctor got all excited.

"Yes. And we'll do it right now, right here in my old bedroom. Okay?"

"Okay..." Ethan then pushed director Ross on the floor, Tracy came to his rescue while the young doctor climbed on the bed, joining Lauren who recently crawled back there.

"Are you sure about what you're doing, Lauren?" Tracy asked as she tried taking care of the old director. Lauren simply nodded before Ethan quickly started kissing her, basically only his tongue to make savage love to her mouth.

"Before we begin the reproduction process, please tell me, where is Noah? Is he alright?" Lauren spoke to her new "love" companion after he finished kissing her.

"Yes, don't worry, he is in the car outside, I sedated him." Reassured, Lauren kept offering her body to the handsome doctor, she passionately kissed the side of his neck while unzipping his pants, pulling his already erect cock out of there. All by herself, she rubbed the tip of his glans against her wet clitoris, then softly slid it inside her pussy. In a missionary position, he began to fuck her, a few thrusts into it, he accelerated, moved deeper into her.

"Let's not go too fast with the *reproduction process* just yet, there's no hurry. I want your mouth, I want to feel it."

"Okay..." They then changed their positions, Lauren sat on her big butt in the middle of the bed while Ethan towered over her, standing on the bed. He pushed his hard dick inside her mouth, then her throat as Tracy observed. Ross was half unconscious at that moment, Ethan probably beat him up before surprising the two girls having sex. The young doctor intensely deep-throat fucked the nearly inexperienced nurse, it got so brutal that he basically skull fucked her the more the action grew in speed. It was as if he tried to take care of his sexual frustrations and to unleash everything on the poor Lauren. Fortunately for her, she seemed to enjoy it, all of it, she had this overexcited, over-aroused expression on her face with her eyes wide opened as she blushed.

But then, as the young doctor seemed to be soon about to ejaculate inside Lauren's throat, Ethan's skin slowly started to change color. He progressively turned whiter and his veins became darker and more visible. It was as if he was getting sick, sucked out his vitality as Lauren sucked his cock.

"What is happening to me? I feel hot all of a sudden, too hot..." While he was still on the brink of cumming, Tracy appeared behind him, standing on top of the bed in his back. She licked his left ear and caressed his testicles.

"Good idea, Lauren, suck him, suck everything you can out of him." Tracy whispered. Just before he ultimately ejaculated, Ethan's cock slid and bounced out of Lauren's mouth, rubbed against her right cheek as he came. He almost immediacy shot multiple warm cum-shots all over the young nurse's face.

When he was done ejaculating, Tracy stopped caressing his balls and used Lauren's unique stereoscope as handcuffs or rope to tie Ethan's hands together very tight behind his back. Lauren licked some of the warm and thick semen that slid down her face, not too far from the side her lips. She swallowed some of the cum as she kept the same overly aroused expression she previously had when she was skull-fucked by the handsome doctor.

"If you really thought we would do all this crazy stuff with you, Ethan, you're a fool." Lauren murmured after eating some of his sperm.

"Yeah, you *won't* be having fun with us and do your fucked up *reproduction* thing. We'll be the ones to have some with you instead." Tracy said.

EPILOGUE

The two nurses pushed the handsome, "handcuffed" doctor inside the still deserted medical clinic of Thunder-Falls. It seemed like the place had stayed more or less completely empty for the few hours that the main medic team had left the building. It was as if time had been suspended, with no Nocturne Nurses to take care of the clinic, no new patients came in and it all suddenly turned into a cold, ghost town. Director Ross and Noah were both conscious again, they tried following the two nurses as much as possible with their slow steps.

"Why bringing me back here?" Ethan asked.

"I still can't believe what you did, dude..." Noah responded to him.

"Look who's talking. You've done some shitty things too." He riffled back at him. Noah looked away and kept his mouth shut, eating his words.

"I wonder as well, why are we bringing him back here, ladies?" Ross asked as well, keeping the question still pending, still up in the air waiting for a concrete answer. Lauren was the only one of the two nurses to actually turn back to him and to acknowledge his question with a smile, but still not worthy of a real answer. Before she could even have the time to turn her head back in front of us, her and the rest of the group were all surprised with the sudden apparition of a man in the clinic as they entered into one of the hallways. This man quickly ran passed them and headed toward the entrance of the building. It was Lauren's ex-boyfriend, Clayton. He seemed all fine and good, very healthy but deeply terrorized as well.

"I'm never coming back here again. Never." He yelled as he ran outside.

"To be honest, I had completely forgotten about him until now... Seems like he didn't enjoy what you did to him too much, Tracy." Lauren said after a short moment of silence.

"Seems like it... I gave him back all his vitality, he should be fine, he was top shape when I examined him in the basement. I wonder why he has no intention in coming back ever..." Tracy responded.

"I definitely want to know the story behind this, at some point." Noah said while looking at the running man outside through one of the windows.

"Same for me..." Ethan quietly said.

***

The handsome, young doctor was thrown into a patient bedroom that looked like a prison cell. It was actually the exact same one that Lauren was forced to stay in way back when she arrived at the clinic following the events at her apartment. Ethan previously greeted her as she waked up and locked her up in this room, this time, Lauren thrown the doctor in there herself, then imprisoned him. Locking up his cell.

"So, you're just gonna leave me here?" Ethan asked Lauren, staring at her in the eyes.

"For now. Until we figure out what we're going to do with you." She answered. The rest of the group had already left the cell and walked away in the hallway. Lauren was the only one who stayed near the locked up patient bedroom. She turned her back to Ethan, she was about to leave as well.

"Come on, do you actually believe what I was planning to do was *this* bad? Okay, alright, the fire was a huge mistake, but think about it, giving birth to more awesome and unique people like you could save the world. I am still a doctor. Saving people is my only purpose." She listened to him until he was done, she didn't know what to say.

***

Next stop, the emergency room where Matthew was treated this morning, it had already been a few hours since the two nurses left him as he was sedated. The patient of the day was in fact still asleep when the crew arrived here. His sick penis had drastically decreased in size, about half of what it previously was during the peak of the crisis. Lauren ran up to him, immediately used her stethoscope to read his heartbeats. After a short moment of listening, she turned to the rest of the group and smiled, she gave them the thumbs up.

117

"Full recovery."

***

When things had settled a little, Noah calmly rested in his own private office within the clinic. He sat in a chair behind his desk, he used his laptop, searched for a specific file. He'd found it, it was the recorded video of Lauren treating her patient.

The last surviving digital copy of this video.

Noah watched for a while, enjoyed it one last time before he chose all by himself to permanently delete it.

***

After the storm, in another spot of the clinic, in the throne room, director Ross and the gorgeous nurse Castle discussed. Both of them stood near the big desk.

"You still called this office of yours your *throne?* I'm not even surprised."

"Thanks for your help, Tracy. I never thought you and the rookie would team-up like you did."

"The girl has the potential to become a decent Nocturne Nurse. I think she'll do great in your clinic."

"I knew for some time now that one of my two doctors hid something from me. I wasn't sure which one, if I had to chose which one would had plotted something as awful as what happened, I would have guessed Noah was the guilty one. I guess I was dead wrong."

"It wasn't the only thing you were wrong about, director..."

"Yeah, I was getting to that... I'm sorry for the trouble that I caused you... I had no idea you were in town, I thought you still worked at your own hospital... I honestly had no idea you were the one under the mask... So many different people currently posses that mask. In the end, I'm glad it was you under it."

"And I totally thought you knew that it was me. I wanted to keep her here as much as possible. But, speaking of the other persons who have it... I have a question, director..."

"Yes? What is it?"

"Why did you forced me to wear it back in the days?" He looked down at the floor after she asked him that painful question.

***

Two days later, Matthew was kept for safety surveillance at the clinic, Lauren examined him one more time in his own patient bedroom during the afternoon.

"I think you'll be ready to go today."

"Really?" Matthew excitingly responded.

"Yes." Sporting a huge smile on her face.

"But now, to be honest, I'm not sure about leaving the clinic anymore..."

"What do you mean?" She said, all curious and confused. After looking at her chest for a second or two, Matthew quickly leaned forward and dove down between her pair of huge tits. He grabbed both of them, caressed them while his cheeks rubbed against her cleavage. Lauren then immediately blushed, raised her arms in the air, unsure what to do next. While she felt a little uncomfortable, she never tried preventing him from touching, never tried getting away. She didn't mind it all, didn't like it, didn't hate it.

"You're such a lovely and caring nurse. I want to stay here forever."

"Well, I don't know about that, I think you'll need to get back home to your wife."

"No, I don't want to..." This was when backup came in, Tracy waited motionless at the entrance of the room, her back leaning against the wall, smiling to the young nurse and her most recent patient.

"Seems like you are starting to get popular around here."

***

During the same afternoon, doctor Ethan Garden reflected on his situation in his cell, he sat at the end of his bed. He waited for people to stop walking in the hallway to get something under the bed, a box, he held it in his hands, looked at it for while before opening it.

A mask and a costume of the stranger with the red crosses were waiting for him within the box.

AFTERWORD

Here we go again!

This is my second time writing a "afterword" section of a book, although that I called it a "postscript" for my first one. It is kind of the same but I decided to go with "afterword" for Nocturne Nurse.

No particular reason except that I thought it sounded a little better and less formal.

Anyway, yes, here we are, I finished my second book. Swirling Depravity, a novelette was my introduction to the world of creating novels, Nocturne Nurse is a novella. So, a similar thing but simply longer. I started with a novelette so I could get my feet wet and began with something very short. It was shorter to write, and it is a lighter, quicker read. I thought it was a good deal for trying myself at writing novels. If you didn't know, I started with writing scripts for comics, I still do, and I still love it but trying different things was something that appealed to me.

Although that making Swirling Depravity was shorter than it took me for Nocturne Nurse, it still took me a while to properly outline it and get it going. But Nocturne Nurse was in the end a real challenge compared to it, I had a clear idea of what I wanted to accomplish despite maybe being a strange idea.

Weird or not, the original idea for this book was not very complex but rather simple. It is my own spin on medical television series drama (having series such as ER, House M.D., among others for example) but done in novelized form and with an honest, real Hentai environment to it. That was an idea I came up with and I thought it could make for a different story. Not that a medical, doctor, or nurse based Hentai story hadn't been done before, no, it's quite a popular genre, but as I said, the idea was to put my own spin on it. My own twist.

To be honest, I wasn't sure I was going to have a new novel out this year. After Swirling Depravity, I was in no rush to come up with a new one right away. But after a few months of simply slowly plotting in my head, this project come to life a lot faster than I originally thought it was going to happen.

Thank you, TGBK, the artist who did the art for the cover page of this novella. I think you did an impressive job on this project and I wish you the very best for the future.

Thanks to Bushinryu as well, the other artist who worked on some of the illustrations for this novella. He did the Tracy Castle artwork that you can see on the back of the book for example. Thanks a lot.

Special thanks to Jim, my partner in crime who helped me a lot again for this project. He is the best beta reader and collaborator I could ever hope to have for writing those kinds of books. Thanks, buddy.

And last not least, thanks to the lovely woman who edited this novella. I love you.

I hope with all my heart that you enjoyed this book.

Thank you for picking it up, either by purchasing it or borrowing it from a friend.

In any cases, thanks a million times for reading it. Until next time...

ENDING CREDITS

Original Concept & Story By: Camille Juteau

Illustrations By:

TGBK (Cover Art)

Bushinryu (Other Illustrations)

Editor: Kellie O'Reilly

Produced By: Seishi

MORE COPYRIGHTS

Copyright © 2019 Seishi & Camille Juteau.
Seishi, Camille Juteau. Nocturne Nurse (A Hentai Novella) Seishi
The same overall copyrights info applies for both the physical copy of this book and the Digital eBook version of it.

ISBN Numbers:
ISBN Number For eBook (Electronic Book) version:
978-0-9958398-3-0

ISBN Number For Paperback (Physical) version:
978-0-9958398-4-7

ISBN 978-0-9958398-4-7

End of the book.

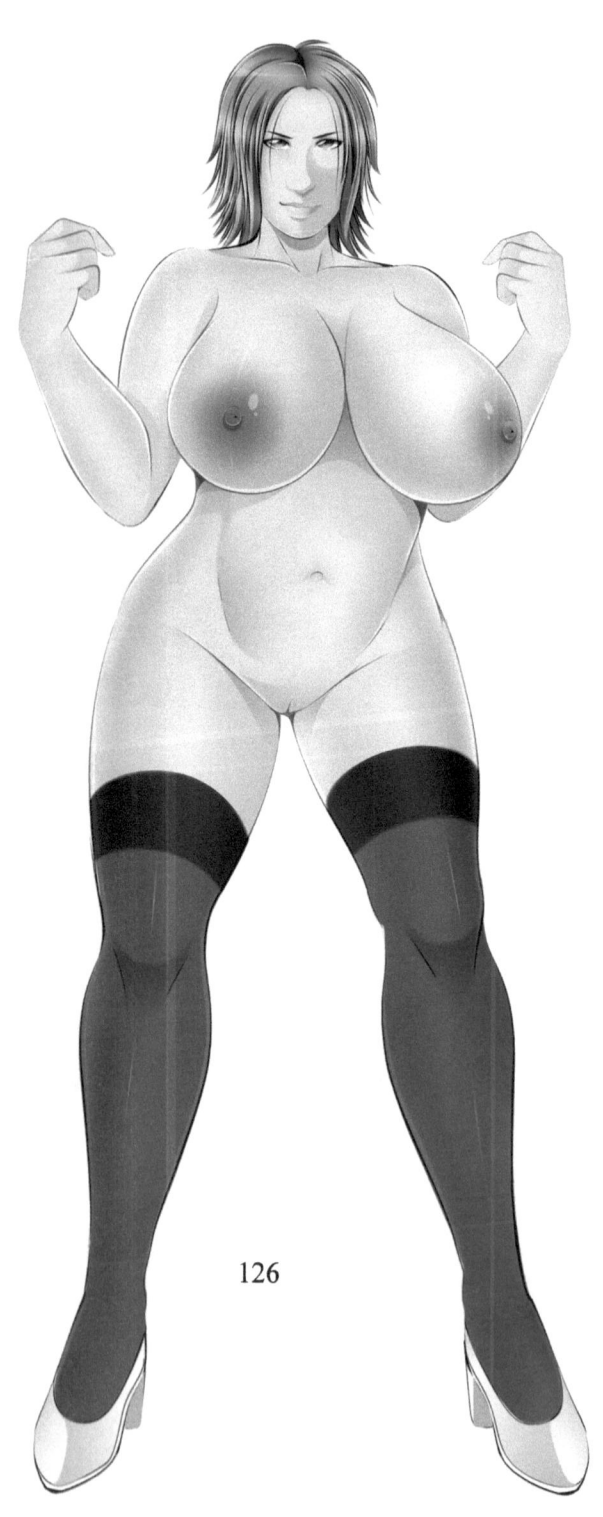

126